THE CASE OF THE
ABANDONED AUSSIE

A Thousand Islands Doggy Inn Mystery

B.R. SNOW

D1572637

Copyright © 2016 B.R. Snow

ISBN: 978-1-942691-05-1

Website: www.brsnow.net/

Twitter: @BernSnow

Facebook: facebook.com/bernsnow

Cover Design: Reggie Cullen

Cover Photo: James R. Miller

Other Books by B.R. Snow

The Damaged Po$$e Series

- American Midnight
- Larrikin Gene
- Sneaker World
- Summerman
- The Duplicates

Other books

- Divorce Hotel
- Either Ore

Acknowledgements

First of all, I'd like to thank all of my readers for their ongoing support and encouragement. I hope you enjoy my new *Thousand Islands Doggy Inn* cozy mystery series. As you will soon figure out, it's an alphabet series that will highlight a specific breed in each book. As such, I guess I better get back to writing. Twenty-six books is a lot, but fortunately, I'm writing about three of my favorite things; dogs, food, and the Thousand Islands. So it doesn't really seem like work at all.

I'd also like to thank Reggie Cullen and Jim Miller for their generosity and creativity. Reggie is my extremely talented cover designer whose work fully captures the essence of each book he works on. Jim is a great photographer whose has kindly agreed to let me use some of his fantastic photos to help showcase the beauty of the Thousand Islands. They both have my ongoing appreciation and respect for all they have done to support me.

As always, I need to thank my wife, Laurie, for her love and support. I couldn't do what I do without you being here.

To the people of the Thousand Islands on both sides of the River.

Chapter 1

Oh, hi.

You caught me by surprise. I was right in the middle of trying to land this smallmouth bass and didn't see you right away.

But I'm delighted you decided to drop in for a visit. And as we like to tell everyone who chooses to stop by our little slice of heaven; thanks for coming and we hope you enjoy your stay.

And since it looks like we're going to be spending some time together, I suppose the best place to start is with me telling you a bit about myself.

First, let's get some of the easy stuff out of the way. My name is Suzy Chandler, and I live in one of the most beautiful locations in the world. It's a magical place called the Thousand Islands that's located on the St. Lawrence River. Now that I think about it, the islands are actually located *in* the River.

But that's probably a distinction without a real difference.

For some of the more geographically challenged, the St. Lawrence connects the Great Lakes to the Atlantic Ocean, a distance about 750 miles and it forms a large portion of the U.S. and Canadian border. But for us who live on either side of the River, when you're out on your boat, the border between our two countries is another one of those distinctions without a real difference.

But just trying telling that to the Coast Guard or Immigration if you happen to get stopped.

The town I live in is, like most small towns, friendly, relatively close-knit, and prone to gossip. During the summer months, the population of Clay Bay, our little town of about 2,000 people often triples due to the influx of tourists and island residents. But when winter arrives, and they can be long and brutal, only the heartiest of our residents remain.

Many people head south to escape the snow and cold, but I, and I'm not alone here, love the winter. I also appreciate where the River is located. If our region were in a climate that was warm year round, the place would be ruined and probably dominated by high-rise condos and a preponderance of umbrella drinks.

Not that I've got anything against umbrella drinks. Or even high rise condos. They both have their place. But that place isn't here.

The long winter that dominates the River with snow and ice gives it a chance to renew and refresh itself. So it can be ready for the arrival of spring and the annual onslaught of people eager for another summer on the River. I consider the winter renewal essential to the long-term future of the St. Lawrence. Winter also does the same thing for me. Coming out of winter, I am battle-tested and ready for whatever life decides to throw at me.

Regarding the question of how I put food on the table, along with my best friend and business partner, Josie, I run the Thousand Islands Doggy Inn, a place we created to provide dogs with the things they deserve; which is the best of everything. And I should also mention that spending one's work day surrounded by boundless, unconditional love isn't a bad way to go. And I know for a fact that it sure beats accounting. Or being a lawyer.

I'm sure you know that my comment about unconditional love was about dogs. Regarding my personal relationship status, I'm single. In fact, at the moment, I'm not even dating. I'm not particularly happy about that, but not torn up about it either. By now, I thought I'd be settled down, but I haven't had the privilege of meeting Mr. Right. Or if I have I somehow missed it. I try not to think about that possibility too often. But I remain quietly confident. He's out there somewhere.

At the risk of sounding immodest, I think it's fair to say that other people would consider me good looking. Not drop dead gorgeous like Josie who makes men tend to forget their names just by looking at them, but I can hold my own in mixed company.

What's that? How old am I?

Nice try.

Only my mother knows how old I am, and she isn't talking. Revealing her daughter's age would divulge too much information about her own math problem.

I'm fluent in French, can cook a bit, enjoy good wine and conversation, and I love bad TV, especially any show that deals with solving a mystery.

Oh yeah, as you probably already figured out, I also like to fish.

And since it's the opening day of the bass season that's exactly what I'm doing at the moment.

I cast towards the edge of shallows and immediately saw the tip of my fishing rod begin to bend. The line tightened, I set the hook with a gentle flick of my wrist and began reeling the fish back towards the boat. Josie placed her rod in a holder attached to the transom, grabbed a net, then scooped the smallmouth bass out of the water.

That's one of the things I love about Josie. She's always there to help me out even when she'd rather be doing something else. Like not fishing.

I grabbed the fish, removed the hook, and gently slid it back into the water. It wiggled its tail for traction then disappeared beneath the water.

"That's nine," Josie said. "What's your secret?"

"I always catch what I'm after," I said, winking at her as I cast my line back into the shallows.

"Except men," Josie said, flashing me a small smile.

"Yeah, well, there is that," I said, checking my bait. "Besides, it's opening day. If you can't catch anything today, you don't deserve to call yourself a fisherman."

"Don't you mean fisherwoman?"

"I tried that," I said, shaking my head. "But it sounds weird."

"Fisherperson?"

I laughed.

"That's even worse."

"Well, this fisher-whatever is going back to trolling for muskie."

I watched Josie head to the stern and cast her line off the back of the boat.

"How many times do I have to tell you?" I said. "October and November are the best months to fish for muskie."

"Hey, they have to eat, right?"

I nodded. If there's one thing I don't argue with Josie about; it's eating.

"I'm pretty sure the muskie aren't waiting until October to grab a snack," she continued. "And the idea of catching a fifty-pound fish is more appealing than messing around with bass, no matter how many you catch. Besides, I love a challenge."

"Knock yourself out," I said, reeling in another bass.

"Nice one," Josie said, scooping the fish out of the water with the net. "Oh, I forgot to tell you. Your mother called this morning and said she was going to stop by later this afternoon."

"Great," I said, frowning.

"Another blind date?"

"Undoubtedly," I said.

"Who's up in the rotation?"

"Well, let's see. Recently Mom's gone lawyer, entrepreneur, doctor, executive. So I'm going to guess lawyer."

4

"You want to do our usual routine?" Josie said, stretching out to enjoy the early morning sun.

"If you're not busy," I said, casting towards the shallows.

"I'm never too busy to watch your love life crash and burn with my own eyes," Josie said, laughing.

"You're one to talk."

"At least I haven't needed any help," Josie said. "My lack of a love life is totally self-inflicted."

"I can ask my mother to fix you up if you like," I said, grinning.

Josie laughed.

"Thanks, but I'll pass. I've seen enough of her taste in men."

My mother.

Just wait until you meet her.

I reeled another bass towards the boat. Again, Josie grabbed the net and scooped the fish out of the water. I removed the hook and gently returned the bass to the water. By now, you've probably figured out that while I'm pretty good at catching fish, I'm even better at letting them go.

My catch and release philosophy stems from one simple fact: I hate the taste of fish.

I know. I've heard it all. Fish is good for me. I should eat more of it. They're packed with protein and nutrients. They keep your brain sharp. Eating fish can help cure depression.

Truth be told, about the only thing I find depressing these days is the prospect of having to eat fish.

Don't even get me started on sushi.

"I'm done," I said, putting my rod away.

I stared out at the open water of the St. Lawrence River. After a few false starts, summer had finally arrived, and I knew that the next five months would be glorious before another long winter arrived. A few hundred feet

5

from the boat something caught my eye, and I grabbed the set of binoculars that went everywhere with me. Josie noticed and followed my eyes.

"What is it?" Josie said.

"I'm not sure," I said, staring through the binoculars. "Whatever it is, it's swimming. Probably a muskrat. Or maybe a mink."

Josie grabbed her pair of binoculars and trained them on the object.

"It's heading right towards us."

"Yeah," I said. "And it's making good time."

"That's not a muskrat, Suzy. It's a dog."

"You're right. It's a puppy. The poor thing looks frantic."

"And very focused on us."

We both watched the puppy continue to paddle its way towards the boat.

"Should we go get him?" Josie said.

"No, let's stay put and let it come to us. If we move the boat, it might freak out even more."

"Okay," Josie said. "It's a good swimmer. I'll grab a towel."

Josie headed to the bow and returned with two large beach towels. I knelt over the edge of the boat, and the puppy swam directly into my arms. I lifted the puppy out of the water and held it against my chest as Josie began toweling its head. The puppy licked both our hands, then sneezed.

"What a gorgeous dog."

"Have you ever see one that wasn't?" Josie said, laughing.

"Well, this one is especially gorgeous. Australian Shepherd, right? Look at those beautiful green eyes. How old do you think it is?"

Josie took the dog and held it up in the air. She removed the towel and examined the tag attached to the elaborate collar it wore.

"Probably around three months. And she's a girl. Her name is Chloe. How are you, Chloe?" Josie looked at me. "She's scared, but she seems fine. We'll get her back to the Inn, and I'll take a good look at her."

When Josie says she'll take a good look at the puppy, she means it. Like every veterinarian I've ever met, she's incredibly devoted to her work and loves dogs almost as much as I do.

And that's a lot of love.

Josie put the dog down, and we laughed as it shook vigorously, spraying water over both of us. I repositioned the towel and held the puppy against my chest. She licked my hand again then nestled its head under my arm.

"You poor thing," I said. "What were you doing all by yourself in the middle of the river?"

The boat jerked and stopped drifting. Josie looked off the stern and saw her fishing rod bending severely in its holder.

"How about that?" Josie said, racing off to grab her rod. "No chance of catching a muskie, huh?"

I watched Josie struggle against the weight of the fish on her line as she reeled it in. As she continued, it became apparent, if it was a muskie, it was of world record size.

"There's a phone number on the collar," I said. "The owner must be frantic."

I turned away from Josie's ongoing battle with the fish, and I grabbed my phone and dialed the number on the dog's collar.

"Uh-oh," Josie said.

"What is it?" I said, staring off into the distance as I waited for the call to connect.

"This ain't no muskie."

"Hang on. It's ringing."

7

"Need you over here, Suzy. Oh, my goodness."

"What is it?" I said, holding the puppy with one arm and the phone against my ear as I walked to the stern. "Dang, nobody is answering."

"Listen," Josie said.

"What is that?"

"Well, I can't be sure, but it sure sounds like a phone ringing," Josie said.

"Yeah, but where?"

"Down there. In the water."

I glanced over the back of the boat and saw the body floating face down.

"Wow. Poor guy. It is a guy, right?"

"Yes, it certainly is. We need to call Jackson."

"Hang on. Let me check something first."

I ended the call, then immediately pressed the redial button. The sound of a phone ringing under the water returned.

"Well," I said. "If there's any good news here, I think we found Chloe's owner."

"What is that stuff floating on the surface near his head?" Josie said.

"That's weird. Is that oil?" I said.

"I don't think it's oil," Josie said, peering down into the water.

"The bigger question is where did all these bees come from?"

Chapter 2

I watched the police boat approach then slow and drift towards us. Still cradling the sleeping Chloe, I waved at Jackson, Clay Bay's Chief of Police. He was someone a lot of people underestimated because he was, in a word, average. Average looks, average build, average intelligence. And because he was content being a small town cop, happy to spend his spare time outdoors and on the River, people often believed he lacked drive. But he was rock-solid and took his responsibilities very seriously.

And Jackson was a very good friend of ours. In fact, we considered him family. He and I had grown up together and he'd once been, what my mother called, *smitten* with me. And he stayed smitten until Josie got her vet license and moved here to join me as co-owner of the Inn. After that, Jackson, along with pretty much every other man who came in contact with her, shifted his affections away from me and focused on Josie.

You might think I'd be offended as the attention I used to attract started to fade, and, at first, perhaps I was a little, but I understand completely. Josie is one of those rare women who seamlessly combines beauty, compassion, and intelligence with a great sense of humor. If she weren't my best friend in the world, perhaps I'd find her threatening or be jealous of how men fall at her feet.

But I doubt it.

Josie's just so darn likable.

And like I said, she loves dogs almost as much as I do.

Next to Jackson in the boat was a young woman I didn't recognize. Josie tied the police boat to ours and stepped back as Jackson and his companion climbed aboard.

"Hi, Josie," Jackson said. "You're looking beautiful as always."

"It's not gonna happen, Jackson," Josie said, grinning.

"You could at least tell me why."

"What can I say, Jackson. You're not my type."

"You got a problem with dating cops?"

"No."

"You don't like my looks?"

"That's not it. I think you're kind of cute."

"You find my personality too big and overpowering?" Jackson said, grinning.

"There you go," Josie said, laughing. "Let's go with that."

"It's a gift. If nothing else, you must find my persistence endearing," he said, then glanced around the boat. "I understand you hooked a big one."

"Yeah, you could say that," Josie said, pointing toward the stern. "He's off the back."

"You didn't touch anything, right?"

"No, we called you right away."

"Good. Hey, Suzy."

"How are you doing, Jackson?"

"Well, since I'm leaving town today, the last thing I need is a dead body to deal with."

"You going on vacation right at the start of the summer season?" I said.

"No, it's a conference in Vegas. Just my luck. Summer finally arrives on the River, and I have to go to the desert. By the way, this is my summer intern, Alice Wonders. Alice, I'd like you meet Suzy and Josie, co-owners of the Thousand Islands Doggy Inn."

I smiled at the attractive young woman who seemed both excited and nervous about what was about to unfold.

"Nice to meet you, Alice," I said, then looked at Jackson. "Since when do you get a summer intern?"

"Ever since your mother called me and asked for a favor."

I glanced back at Alice.

"Do you know my mother?"

"Yes, I've met her a few times."

"Please accept my condolences."

Alice laughed.

"She's okay. Maybe a little quirky," Alice said, relaxing a bit.

"I guess quirky is a word for it. Let me guess. My mother is dating your... divorced father?"

"My uncle."

"Oooh, you were so close," Josie said, laughing.

"He's my dad's brother. Your mom was at a family dinner a couple of months ago, and I mentioned I was majoring in Criminology. So here I am." She snuck a cautious peek towards the stern. "I've never seen a dead body before."

"Your mother made me an offer I couldn't refuse," Jackson said.

"Just because she used to be the Mayor and is on the Town Council doesn't mean you have to agree to do everything she tells you to," I said.

"Yeah, right," Jackson said, chuckling. "I don't see you saying no to her very often."

"I say no to her all the time," I said. "But it just doesn't register. She has trouble processing the word no."

Jackson nodded and glanced out over the water.

"That reminds me. Your mother was speeding again last night."

"I hope you gave her a ticket," I said.

"No, I couldn't catch her. Her new one is incredibly fast. What kind of car is it?"

"I don't know. I haven't seen her this week." I looked at Alice. "My mother changes cars like other people change their socks."

"I don't want to deal with it," Jackson said. "In fact, I hate the thought of it. But I may have to do something. What do you think I should do if I have to arrest your mother?"

"Call for backup."

Jackson laughed and shook his head.

"Okay, let's have a look," he said, heading towards the stern. He noticed the puppy. "Got yourself another dog?"

I explained Chloe's arrival and how the phone number on the collar matched the one on the phone of the dead man floating in the water.

"That's odd," Jackson said as he scanned the open water. "No sign of a boat?"

"No," I said.

"I'm going to flip him over," Jackson said. "I know you two are veterans with this sort of thing but are you sure you want to see this on your first day, Alice?"

"That's why I'm here, right?" Alice said, glancing nervously around the boat at Josie and me.

"Actually, I thought you'd be spending the summer watching me write speeding tickets and deal with drunk tourists."

Jackson leaned over the stern and pulled the body closer. He removed the hook from Josie's rod and handed it to her. He then grabbed the man's shoulder and flipped the body over.

"Hey, I know this guy," Jackson said. "Robert Crawford. He owns Candyland Island."

We stared down at the man's face. Alice wretched, staggered to the other side of the boat and threw up. Fortunately, she managed to hit the water. Josie and I continued to study the body closely.

12

"The name sounds familiar," Josie said.

"He was a candy magnate," Jackson said. "He's owned Candyland Island for a while, but I don't think he visited very often."

"It doesn't look like he's been in the water very long," I said.

"No, you're right," Jackson said. "There's no bloating. He looks pretty fresh."

"For a dead guy," Josie said.

"Well, sure. That goes without saying. No visible wounds or signs of a struggle. My guess is that Mr. Crawford was going too fast, probably last night. Then he hit something, probably a shoal, and he and the dog got tossed overboard. That would explain the lack of a boat."

"So he drowned?" Alice said as she snuck another quick peek at the body.

"I reckon so," Jackson said. "We lose a few people every summer. The River is a dangerous place when people don't treat it with respect."

"But what's that stuff surrounding his head?" Josie said.

"I'm not sure," Jackson said. "But those bees sure do seem to like it."

Chapter 3

I slowed the boat as we approached the dock. Josie hopped out and secured the lines. The boat gently rocked as I climbed out with Chloe nestled under one arm. I set her down on the dock, and she cocked her head at me and wagged her tail.

"Looks like you've made a friend," Josie said.

"She's incredible," I said, leaning down to rub her head.

"Uh-oh, I know that look."

"What?"

"That's your *I've got a new dog look*."

"Well, she is homeless at the moment," I said.

Josie laughed and started walking down the dock in the direction of the Inn. I looked down at Chloe.

"You want a ride, or would you like to walk?"

Not waiting for an answer, I bent down and picked her up, then followed Josie down the dock.

As we walked up the hill that led to the Inn, the place where Josie and I spent the majority of our time, I noticed a sleek foreign car in the parking lot next to the main building. My mother spied us approaching, and she climbed out. The way the car door opened, it looked more like she was *escaping*. She clamored to her feet, brushed the hair away from her face, and, hands on hip, beamed at us. For her, she was casually dressed. Forest green silk blouse accented with a yellow scarf; open toe pumps that probably cost more than our monthly dog food bill; and jeans that looked like they'd been spray painted on.

I had to admit it. She looked magnificent. Once again, I crossed my fingers and hoped that my aging process would go half as well.

"Good morning, Mom."

"Hello, darling. Whoa. What is that smell? Please tell me you haven't been fishing."

"Opening day of the bass season, Mom."

She shook her head, obviously disappointed with my ongoing reluctance to accept her definition of what constituted appropriate female behavior.

"Hi, Josie. Don't tell me she's dragged you into the world of lures and fish guts."

Josie laughed.

"What can I say, Mrs. C?"

"You can say no," my mother said, then looked at me. "I blame her father."

My mother looked skyward and blew a kiss towards the heavens. Even though my dad had been gone a long time, every time his name came up she always took a moment to pay tribute to him. And it always caused a lump in my throat.

"It was a way for us to get out of the house without you tagging along," I said, forcing a smile.

"Funny, darling. Well, what do you think of my new toy?"

I gave the strange looking car a quick glance and shrugged.

"It's nice. I guess."

"Nice? It's a Ferrari, darling."

"Italian, right?"

"Good guess," Josie said.

"I've raised a Philistine," my mother said, rolling her eyes. "Who's the little fur ball?"

15

"This is Chloe."

I offered the puppy to my mother who held up both palms in protest.

"Silk blouse, darling. Don't you have enough dogs?"

"I'll never have enough dogs, Mom. Isn't she gorgeous?"

"Yes, she is. Where did you get her?"

"She used to be owned by Robert Crawford."

"She's Bob's dog?"

"She was."

My mother gave me her *I'm waiting for more* look. So I told her about our adventure that morning. When I finished, she nodded with a sad frown on her face.

"That's too bad. I always liked Bob."

"Liked how?" I said. It was my turn to give her the *I'm waiting* look.

"After his divorce, we dated a bit."

"I see," I said. "What was he like?"

"Darling, you're not asking me to kiss and tell, are you?"

"Definitely not," I said, feeling my face flush. The thought of my mother sharing details of her romantic liaisons made my skin crawl. "I was referring to his personality. You know, his overall demeanor."

"He was… driven. It was like he was on a mission to conquer everything that got in his way."

"I see. And did he?"

"What? Conquer me?" she said, laughing. "Darling, no one conquers me. You know better than that."

She was right. I did know better. Score a point for Mom.

"Okay, moving on to new business," my mother said. "Tomorrow night. 7:30 at Tondeuse. I've found you a delightful young lawyer from New York. He's in town for a few days, and I know the two of you will hit it off."

16

"Ah, Mom." As soon as I said it, I wanted to kick myself for sounding like a whiny teenager.

"There's no need to thank me," she said. "But be on time, and play nice. Oh, Sammy Jenkins is coming in today for an interview."

"Who?"

I looked at Josie. She checked her phone and nodded.

"Two o'clock. I have no idea how it got on my calendar."

"I had Jill put it there," my mother said.

Jill was one of our staff members at the Inn. She was bright, personable, and a very hard worker. Her only shortcoming was that she was scared to death of my mother. Of course, Mom knew this and took full advantage.

"I want you to take good care of Sammy," my mother said. "He's a good kid. Just not the sharpest tool in the shed if you get my drift."

"Another favor to a friend?"

"Darling, when you have as many friends as I do, you get to do a lot of favors."

She reached out and gently touched my face, then rubbed Chloe's head.

"Cute dog. Look, I need to run. Don't forget. Tomorrow. 7:30. Now go take a shower, darling. You stink."

She waved goodbye, climbed back into her car, and roared down the driveway. I watched until the car disappeared amid a cloud of dust.

"They should name a hurricane after her," Josie said.

"No, what they should do is name the whole hurricane *season* after her," I said.

Inside, the Inn hummed with its usual morning hustle and bustle punctuated by the occasional bark. I handed Chloe to Josie, who took her into one of the exam rooms. I chatted with a couple of regular customers sitting with their dogs who were getting their annual checkup. Another

17

couple was going away for the weekend and were boarding their black lab, a magnificent animal we loved having around. I sat down behind the check-in desk and reviewed the daily log. Twelve boarders, most of them regulars. Nineteen vet appointments. Josie had a long day ahead of her. Seventeen rescue dogs, up from fifteen the day before. I waited for Jill to finish a phone call, then nodded for her to follow me into my office.

"Where did the two new rescues come from?" I said.

"I found them last night," Jill said. "I was watering my garden when they wandered into my yard."

"No tags?"

"No. So I brought them in. They're sharing a condo. And I updated the website with their picture and descriptions."

"Good. But we're getting pretty close to capacity on the rescue side, so let's organize an adoption day for next Saturday."

"You got it," Jill said. "And there's somebody here to see you. He says he's here to interview for the summer handler job."

"The one my mother had you schedule?" I said, glancing at my watch.

"Yeah. I'm sorry about doing that without checking with you first. But your mom scares the bejeezus out of me."

"Me too," I said, laughing. "Don't worry about it. He's a little early, isn't he?"

"He's a little something," Jill said.

Josie entered carrying Chloe. She handed me the puppy, who started licking my face.

"She looks fine," Josie said. "Jill, could you see if you can track down her vet so we can make sure she's had all her shots?"

"Sure. What a cutie," Jill said, scratching one of Chloe's ears. "You want me to put her in one of the condos?"

"No, she's staying right here with me," I said.

18

I caught Jill and Josie sharing a smirk.

"So I'm a soft touch," I said, cradling Chloe. "Our two o'clock is here."

"Really? Well, either he's eager to get started, or he can't tell time. Let's get it done now before my day's shot."

We walked back into the reception area and gestured to the young man sitting in a chair near the window. He shuffled in our direction and stood on the customer side of reception.

"Hi. I'm Sammy. I think I'm a little early."

"Not if you're in Nova Scotia," I said, smiling.

Confused, he glanced back and forth between Josie and me, then spied a glass jar on the counter.

"Are these for anybody?" Sammy said as he stuck his hand in the jar.

"Sure, help yourself," I said, watching him taking a bite. I glanced at Josie, who continued staring at the young man.

"It's a nice way to welcome your customers," Sammy said, chewing.

"Yeah," Josie said. "We like to think so."

"Good cookies," he said.

"Uh, Sammy," I said. "Those are dog biscuits."

"Really? They're not bad," he said, then frowned. "They can't hurt me, can they?"

"No, I think you'll be fine," Josie said. "But if you develop an urge to start scratching and licking yourself, be sure to let us know."

Chapter 4

I sat on the front porch holding the sleeping Chloe as I waited for Josie to finish her last appointment. I wasn't happy about what we were about to do, but there was no way around it.

"Maybe they won't want you," I said as I stroked her head.

I looked up at the sound of a car pulling into the parking lot and waved to the driver. Jackson climbed out; then his knees buckled when the dog that had been sitting in the passenger seat scrambled out the open door past him. Jackson shook his head as he closed the car door and followed the dog onto the front porch.

"Hi, Jackson. Hey, Sluggo," I said, rubbing the bulldog's head and ducking the trails of saliva the dog was shaking off its jowls.

For the moment Sluggo was more interested in Chloe, who'd woken and was staring at the drooling beast that was inching closer. They exchanged looks and sniffs then Sluggo lost interest and sat down and waited for me to continue rubbing his head. He rolled over, and his long tongue dropped onto the deck as soon as I ran my fingernails down his belly

"Sluggo, have you no shame?" Jackson said, sitting down next to me.

Josie stepped outside, immediately spotting the bulldog.

"Sluggo, how's my boy?" she said, kneeling down to take over belly scratching duties. Sluggo kicked all four legs in the air and snorted with delight. She glanced up. "Hi, Jackson."

"Any chance I can get one of those?" he said, grinning.

"Just as soon as you get four legs," Josie said, standing up. "You ready to go?"

"I guess," I said.

"Where are you girls off to?"

"Candyland Island to see which family member is going to take Chloe," Josie said.

"Oh, an evening with the rich and famous. You're moving up in the world."

"It's not an evening," I said. "We're just going to make sure that Chloe will be in good hands, then we're leaving."

"By the way, I talked with Freddie and the death is being listed as an accidental drowning."

"Did you find out what the stuff we saw in the water was?" Josie said.

"Yeah. It was maple syrup," Jackson said.

"That's weird. I guess that explains the bees," I said.

"That was a lot of syrup," Josie said.

"Maybe the guy liked his maple syrup. After all, he was a candy magnate."

"Any sign of the boat?" I said.

"No, nothing. Not even a piece of debris or a boat cushion," Jackson said.

"Don't you find that a bit odd, Jackson?" I said, glancing at Josie.

"Yes, indeed," Josie said. "Something about it does seem odd."

"Yes," I said, nodding. "Downright suspicious."

"Here we go," Jackson said, shaking his head. "Look, both of you know it wouldn't take much for a boat to disappear, especially if it were near the channel when it hit whatever it did. It's probably miles downriver in a hundred feet of water."

"I don't know," I said, shaking my head. "If the boat was in the channel in deep water, why did we find his body in the shallows?"

"Because he floated?" Jackson said. "Why are you two always doing this?"

21

"Doing what?" Josie said.

"Poking your nose where it doesn't belong and looking for conspiracies where there aren't any."

"We are not," I said, protesting. I looked at Josie and shrugged. "Well, maybe once in a while. But you have to admit that it's odd that a guy who'd lived on the River for years would drown like that."

"I'll admit nothing of the sort," Jackson said. "It happens. Maybe he had too much to drink. Maybe he got distracted and forgot where he was."

"Maybe," I said. "But something doesn't seem right. And what about Chloe?"

"Who?" Jackson said.

"Her," I said, nodding at the sleeping puppy. "She's a good swimmer, but the idea of her paddling alone out there all night is pretty hard to believe."

"Maybe she was on a piece of driftwood. Or a boat cushion. Maybe she just has a strong survival instinct," Jackson said, growing more agitated by the minute. "How would I know?"

"I think the whole thing is very suspicious," I said.

"Me too," Josie said.

"Okay, go ahead and play detective. Knock yourself out. But try to stay out of trouble while I'm gone, and don't annoy anybody, especially the tourists. And don't try to arrest anybody."

"What trouble could we possibly get into, Jackson?" I said.

Jackson looked at both of us, then shook his head.

"I'll be back in a few days. If you need anything while I'm gone, you've got my number. And you be a good boy, Sluggo."

With that, Jackson gave Sluggo one last pet and headed towards his car. Josie and I got Sluggo set up in his condo and headed for the dock. We climbed aboard, and Chloe hopped up on the seat next to me.

22

"I called Freddie this afternoon," Josie said, removing her sunglasses.

"And what did our favorite Medical Examiner have to say?"

"Well, first he asked me again if I wanted to work part-time for him."

"Why not?" I said, "You are licensed."

"If I'd wanted to work on people, I would have stayed in med school."

"Then why did you even bother to get your ME license?"

Josie shrugged. "It was something to do. And it taught me that I liked dealing with dead people even less than I did with the sick ones."

I laughed. "So what did Freddie have to say?"

"After I turned down the job offer, we did our usual dance. He asked me out; I said no. Then we finally got around to talking about the deceased Mr. Crawford."

"And?"

"Just like Jackson said. Accidental drowning, no signs of a struggle. No visible wounds."

"What about the maple syrup?"

"Freddie said it was odd, but not any real evidence of anything. And since the family didn't want an autopsy and the police were satisfied he wasn't a victim of foul play, they're going ahead with the cremation."

"That was fast," I said, stroking Chloe's head.

"Families deal with death in different ways."

"Yeah, I guess," I said. "But something about this bugs me."

"Me too."

"Let's keep our eyes open when we get there."

"Well, if I'm going to need to do that, I need a nap."

She stretched out on the back seat and closed her eyes. Chloe, another victim to the fresh air and soft purr of the engine, was also sound asleep. I stifled a yawn as I pulled on a sweater to keep the cool evening breeze at bay.

23

Chapter 5

There aren't really a thousand islands. The number totals 1,864, but the Thousand Islands has a much better ring to it and works better on the tourist brochures. When I was a kid, I wondered why they hadn't rounded up and called it the Two Thousand Islands, then I'd decided the area probably got its name before anyone had gotten around to counting all of them.

Candyland Island was like the majority of the other Thousand Islands; comprised of granite and dominated by pine and cedar trees. But unlike a lot of the other islands, Candyland was big. Not as big as Howe Island, the largest that was almost thirty miles long. But certainly big enough to handle the Crawford family. And probably everyone else who worked for the deceased magnate's candy company. The island fronted the main shipping channel of the St. Lawrence Seaway, and from the water it was impressive. But it wasn't until I steered the boat away from the Channel toward the back of the island that the grandeur of the place became evident.

A large stone and wood boathouse with more dock space than some local towns offered provided ample parking. All the slips in the boathouse were filled with a wide variety of boats and other watercraft, so I eased the boat along the dock that extended off the front of the boathouse. Both Josie and Chloe woke up at the same time, and Josie hopped out to tie the boat off. Chloe, obviously familiar with her surroundings, hopped from the boat onto the dock and sat down waiting for me.

"Okay," I said, climbing onto the dock. "Let's go meet the Crawfords."

Chloe trotted down the dock and out the boathouse onto a stone trail that led up to the main house. We followed, taking in our surroundings as we walked along the trail.

"How much money do you think this guy had?" Josie said, whistling when she saw the massive, manicured lawn.

"A lot more than you and me."

"That's not saying much," she said, laughing.

"Well, how about a lot more than my mother?"

"There you go," Josie said, watching as Chloe sniffed the lawn for a favorite spot, then squatted to pee. "Good girl. You know, I was watching her around the Inn earlier. That dog is scary smart."

"Yeah," I whispered.

"What's the matter?"

"I'm having separation anxiety," I said.

Josie snorted. "You've had the dog for twelve hours."

"What can I say? We've bonded."

"Can I help you?"

We both turned in the direction of the voice. A good looking tall man wearing work coveralls stained with sweat and grass cuttings was standing behind us holding a shovel. He stared at us with a curious expression, not sure who we were or why we were here. Then he fixated on Josie and slowly took her in with his eyes. Even though I wasn't the object of his stare, I still found it a bit creepy. As usual, Josie waited it out and returned the stare. When it became apparent she wasn't going to flirt back his eyes shifted to the horizon.

Chloe raced across the lawn and put her front paws up on the man. He smiled, bent down, and stroked the dog's fur.

"Well, look at what we have here. I was afraid we'd lost you."

Chloe sat down and glanced back and forth at all three of us.

"You came over here to bring Chloe back?"

"More or less," I said. "Should I call you Mr. Crawford?"

"Hah, that'll be the day," he said, laughing. "I'm Carl. The gardener."

25

"I'm Suzy. This is Josie."

"Nice to meet you, Carl," Josie said.

"Nice to meet you, Josie," he said, on the verge of another outburst of overt leering. "They're all up at the house. C'mon, I'll lead the way."

"We hate intruding," I said. "Given the circumstances. But we thought they'd be worried sick about Chloe."

Carl the Gardener laughed. "The only thing this group worries about is missing happy hour." When his joke didn't elicit any response from us, he shook his head and forced a small smile. "You've never been to the island before, have you?

"No," I said.

"Well, buckle up," he said, walking up the steps toward the house. "You're in for a wild ride."

Confused, I looked at Josie, who shrugged. We followed him up the steps that led to a wraparound verandah offering a magnificent view of the River. He opened the front door and gestured for us to enter. We stepped inside the wood, stone, and glass house that seemed one part hotel, one part museum. Before we had a chance to finish taking everything in, a young woman burst through a wooden door and headed towards us.

"I couldn't care less what you want!" she screamed over her shoulder as she stormed past us and out the front door.

"That was Roxanne," Carl said.

"Daughter?" I said.

"No," Carl the Gardener said, chuckling.

"Granddaughter?"

"No. Girlfriend," he said.

"Ex-girlfriend," Josie said.

"Well, sure. That goes without saying," Carl said. "C'mon, follow me."

Through a large picture window that dominated one side of the foyer, I watched Roxanne come to a stop next to a large swimming pool. She stripped down to a small bikini and stretched her arms over her head. To me, it looked like she was posing, probably out of habit since there was no one else around, then she dove in and began doing laps. She was no Josie, but if you buy into the stereotype of what the young girlfriend of a rich older man should look like, she certainly fit the job description.

Carl took a quick look at the pool and shook his head, then led us into a library dominated by large wooden bookshelves and a stone fireplace.

"Roxanne, I told you I don't want to discuss it," a woman snapped as she glanced up from the stack of papers in her lap. "Oh, it's you. What do you want, Carl?"

"You have guests," Carl said, unperturbed by the woman's demeanor.

The woman studied Josie and me, then noticed Chloe, who wanted nothing to do with her and stayed firmly planted against my leg, growling under her breath.

"What is that dog doing here?"

"Isn't she yours?" I said as I reached down and picked Chloe up.

"It was Mr. Crawford's dog," she said as she looked down and started scrolling through her phone.

I looked at Josie who was not impressed by the woman's rudeness.

"Whom should I speak with about Chloe?" I said.

The woman glanced up, considered the question, then shrugged.

"I have no idea. That would be a question for a *family* member."

"Where would I find a member of the family?"

The woman again glanced up, thought about my question, then shook her head.

"There's no one from the family here at the moment. But Mrs. Crawford will be here tomorrow if you'd like to come back."

27

"I thought Mr. Crawford was divorced," I said.

"He was," the woman said. "But Mrs. Crawford was allowed to keep the last name as part of the settlement. She says it opens doors for her."

"I see," I said. "I guess we could come back tomorrow."

"Please do," the woman said, again focused on her phone. "Stay for dinner."

"Excuse me?" I said, confused.

One minute she can barely acknowledge our presence, the next she's inviting us to dinner?

"Dinner. Tomorrow night," the woman said, forcing a smile at us. "You do eat dinner, right?"

"I've been known to dabble," Josie said.

"Then it's settled," she said. "Besides, every minute you spend talking with her is one less the rest of us will have to deal with. Let's say 7:30."

"Okay," I said, rubbing Chloe's head. "That sounds like a plan."

"No," she said, holding up a stack of papers and waving them in my direction. "This is a plan. Tomorrow night is dinner." She glanced toward the far side of the room. "George, get in here."

A moment later, a harried man in his fifties burst through a side door and hustled until he was standing right in front of her chair.

"Yes, Rosaline?"

"These numbers can't possibly be right," she said. "Look, just because we're stuck on this infernal island doesn't mean you're on vacation."

Infernal? It looked pretty good to me.

"George, I'm not going to tell you again," Rosaline said, continuing her harangue. "No drinking during the day."

"But I wasn't-"

"Really? Then explain this to me," she said, pointing at a page. She glanced up and seemed surprised to see us still there. "Tomorrow night. 7:30."

I glanced at Josie, and we quietly left the library. Outside on the front porch, we found Carl sitting in an Adirondack chair staring out at the River.

"Are you folks having fun?" he said, unable to keep the grin off his face.

"Who is that woman?" I said.

"Rosaline? She's Mr. Crawford's Chief Operating Officer. At least she was. Right now, I'm sure she's trying to figure out what role she'll have going forward. Or if she'll have any role after Mrs. Crawford gets here."

"She's horrible," Josie said.

"This is one of her good days," Carl said. "And compared to Mrs. Crawford, she's an absolute delight. Too bad you didn't get a chance to meet her. She's the sort of person who gives humans a bad name."

"We'll meet her tomorrow night at dinner," Josie said.

"You're coming back for dinner?" Carl said, beaming at Josie. "That's wonderful."

He gave Josie *the look*. Definitely creepy. On occasion, I envied the attention Josie received from men. This wasn't one of those times.

We excused ourselves and headed down the long set of steps that led back to the boathouse. Josie untied the lines and hopped in as I started the boat and backed out.

"That was special," I said, shaking my head.

"Wow," Josie said. "You sure you want to come back?"

"No, but I think we owe the family the chance to decide what they want to do with Chloe. And something about this still bothers me."

"Maybe Crawford was just trying to get away from Rosaline," Josie said, laughing.

29

"Suicide by drowning?"

"Hey, it could happen."

Chapter 6

Josie came into the living room wearing black jeans and a brown silk top that fit so well it looked hand-tailored. I knew it wasn't since I'd been standing right next to her when she spied it on a rack at our favorite discount store and had snatched it before I or any of the other bargain hunters had the chance to grab it. Looking at her now, I knew the blouse had gone to the right person.

Josie twirled in her open-toed sandals and posed for me.

"What do you think?" she said, breaking her pose to bend down and pet Chloe.

"I think you won't have to buy a drink all night," I said, shaking my head. "Life is so unfair. Nobody should look that good."

She laughed and picked Chloe up and scratched behind one of her ears. Chloe melted.

"Are you ready?" she said.

"Yeah, but we need to wait for Sammy. He's agreed to keep an eye on the place."

"You mean to keep an eye on Chloe, don't you?"

"She's such a little girl," I said, taking Chloe from Josie. "We can't leave her alone all night."

"You're such a soft touch," Josie said.

We both turned to the door when we heard the knock. I opened it, and Sammy stepped inside. He gave me a quick once over and smiled.

"Nice outfit," he said. Then he looked at Josie. I can't be sure, but I think I saw his knees buckle. He coughed nervously and stammered. "Y-you look good, too, Doc."

"Call me Josie."

"Okay, J-Josie."

I laughed and handed Chloe to him.

"We're out of here," I said. "Remember to keep her water bowl filled. She should let you know when she needs to go out, but keep an eye on her. She's still getting adjusted to the place. Don't give her *any* people food. But she can have a couple of her cookies later. And if you get hungry, there's a fresh box of dog biscuits in the cupboard."

Sammy flushed with embarrassment and stared down at the floor.

"I'm just kidding, Sammy. Don't worry about it; people make that mistake all the time. Help yourself to anything in the fridge. You have both our numbers so call if anything happens. We should be back by eleven at the latest."

"At least one of us will be," Josie said, grinning at me.

"Don't start."

We headed outside, hopped in my SUV and made our way down the driveway and onto Route 12 that would take us to Tondeuse, by far our favorite restaurant in the area. Eight minutes later, I pulled into the parking area outside the restaurant. We entered, exchanged pleasantries with the hostess, then headed to the bar. We both ordered white wine and glanced around while we waited for our drinks. I exchanged waves with several people, then looked at Josie.

"Okay, we'll do the usual," I said. "If this guy is a total loser, I'll text you."

"Just remember to do it before you order," she said, taking a sip of wine. "I'm starving. And if you don't need me at your table, I'll just eat out here."

"Got it," I said, standing up. "Wish me luck."

I grabbed my glass of wine and tossed a quick wave goodbye over my shoulder. The hostess led me to my table where my blind date was already waiting. He stood up and shook hands with me, then we sat down.

"Call me Jerry," he said.

"Nice to meet you, Jerry," I said, checking him out. He was good looking in a corporate-climber kind of way. A bit too manicured for my taste, bathed in cologne, and his skin tone had tanning bed written all over it. But at least he appeared somewhat athletic. I couldn't see him with a fishing rod in his hand, but it looked like he could at least handle the outdoors. Overall, not a bad first impression.

I know what you're thinking. I was being incredibly judgemental, especially about someone I'd just met. But if you'd seen some of the creatures my mother has set me up with in the past, you'd be judgemental, too. My mother calls it one of my major personality flaws. I consider it an essential defense mechanism. It's just one more thing where we've agreed to disagree.

"Your mother was right," he said. "You're gorgeous."

"Well, I wouldn't put too much stock in what she says. She's a drinker."

He laughed. Too loud. And for far too long.

"No, really," he said, placing both hands on top of mine. "You're incredible."

I waited a few seconds, then pulled my hands away and used them to brush the hair away from my face. I did my best to make it a subtle move, but I think Jerry got the message. He leaned back in his chair and studied my face. I forced a smile and waited.

"Your mother tells me that you own a hotel for dogs," he said, chuckling.

I felt the hairs on the back of my neck rise.

"Why does that strike you as funny?"

"It's not funny," he said, unable to maintain eye contact. "It's just... unusual. Yes, that's it, unusual."

"It's a lot more than just a boarding hotel. We run a full-service veterinary operation. And we operate a dog rescue program."

"Is there any money in dogs?" he said, then took a sip of his martini and stared at me over the top of the glass.

"Why would that matter?" I said, reaching underneath the table for my phone.

"Because money's important," he said, shrugging as if the answer was obvious. "Isn't it important to you?"

"I have money," I said. "What I don't have is enough dogs."

I glanced down and texted Josie the message: KMN. I slid the phone back into my purse, then picked up my wine glass.

Oblivious to my texting, Jerry stared off into the distance, his face in profile. I realized that while he seemed to be in deep thought, he was posing for me.

"How many dogs do you have?" he said, refocusing on me with a small smile.

"All in?"

"Yeah, sure. All in," Jerry said, shrugging.

"Between the temporary boarders, permanent residents, and the rescues, today's count is twenty-nine."

"Twenty-nine?" he said, laughing until he coughed. He composed himself and wiped his mouth. "And I thought cat ladies were supposed to be the crazy ones."

"I beg your pardon," I said, making a mental note to have a serious chat with my mother. She had outdone herself this time.

"No offense," he said, draining his martini. "So how long do you keep the rescues before you euthanize them?"

"What?"

"You know, put them to sleep. Isn't that what you do with dogs nobody wants? Isn't that the *humane* thing to do?"

Before I could reach across the table and slap his smug face, Josie approached the table.

"Hey, Suzy," she said, grinning. "Why didn't you tell me you were coming here tonight? We could have ridden together." She caught the scowl on my face but didn't miss a beat. She turned to Jerry and held out her hand.

"Hi, I'm Josie. Suzy's business partner."

Jerry took her extended hand and gently shook it. Stunned by her, he stammered out a hello.

"W-won't you join us?" he said, pointing at the empty chair next to mine.

"Don't mind if I do. I'm starving," Josie said as she sat down. "So, what you are two talking about?"

"Dog euthanasia," I said, taking a sip of wine.

"Not while I'm sitting at the table we're not," she said, glaring at Jerry.

"I just asked the question of when you put rescue dogs to sleep," Jerry said.

"If we ever decide we need to put a dog to sleep, we'll just bring it to dinner with a lawyer," I said.

"Oooh, good one," Josie said.

"Let's say we all just take a deep breath and start over, shall we?" Jerry said. "I'm sorry I asked."

"So you're a lawyer," Josie said.

"Yeah," Jerry said. "Mostly financial law. Some corporate stuff. I work out of New York, but I occasionally get up here in the summer." He glanced up at a man approaching the table. "Well, what a surprise. Look who's here."

"Hey, Jer, what's up?"

I glanced up at the man and waited. He could have come from the same mold as the dog-killer sitting across from me. Another lawyer I decided.

"Frederick Naylor, I'd like you to meet Suzy and Josie. They own a hotel for dogs."

"Nice to meet you, ladies," he said, sitting down across from Josie. "Is there any money in that?"

"Millions," Josie said, wet-noodling the man's handshake.

"Man, she wasn't kidding," Frederick said, looking at Jerry. "She's gorgeous."

Jerry flinched, but it was too late. The damage was done. Josie and I looked at each other and scowled.

"Who wasn't kidding?" I said, looking back and forth at them.

"Geez, Frederick," Jerry said. Then he looked at me and shrugged. "Okay, you caught me. Your mother told me about your little first-date game and how Josie manages to show up unexpectedly when things aren't going well. I thought I'd try to outflank you by inviting Frederick along."

"Well," I said, taking a sip of wine. "I have to give you a point for your creativity."

"That has to be worth something, right?"

"Not much," I said.

Jerry turned in his chair and snapped his fingers at the waitress to get her attention.

"Don't do that," I said. "That is not how you treat people. And she's a friend of ours."

"Sorry," Jerry said, glaring at me. "I'd just like to order another drink."

"Yeah, that should help," I snapped.

"This is going very well," Josie said, not looking up from her menu.

"It certainly is," Frederick said, unable to take his eyes off Josie.

"Put it in neutral, Frederick," I said.

"No, I'm serious," he said. "Josie, you're incredible. Those tight black jeans really work on you. And that silk blouse goes great with your skin tone. What shade of brown is that?"

Josie glanced up from her menu, took a quick look at one of the sleeves and said, "Spring mud, I think." She went back to her menu.

"Well, you look fantastic," Frederick said, nudging Jerry in the ribs. "Say, what's black and brown and would look great on a lawyer?"

"A Rottweiler," I said, not bothering to look up from my menu.

Josie snorted with laughter and closed her menu.

"Suddenly, I'm not hungry," she said.

"You know, I'm feeling the same way." I looked across the table at the crestfallen Jerry. "If you gentlemen will excuse us, I think we might call it a night."

"How about a raincheck?" Jerry said.

"Doubtful," I said as I stood up and grabbed my purse. "But it was nice meeting you."

"Yeah," Jerry said. "Your mother warned me. She said you were a tough one to crack."

"What can I say, Jerry? I'm the macadamia nut of dating."

We waved goodbye and left them at the table squabbling with each other.

"I'm still starving," Josie said.

"Me, too. Let's go eat in the bar."

"Are you worried they'll see us?" Josie said, nodding back at the table.

"Not in the least."

"A Rottweiler," Josie said, laughing. "That was a good one."

"I wasn't joking."

"I know. That's what made it funny."

Chapter 7

I worked my way through a Greek salad as I watched Josie devour two dozen steamed clams. I cringed every time she slurped down one of the nasty creatures, but I couldn't resist dipping my bread in the garlic butter sauce.

"You sure you don't want to try one of these?" she said, simultaneously offering me a clam and dipping a piece of bread in the sauce.

"If it's from the sea, it's not for me," I said, shaking my head.

"You don't know what you're missing," she said, tossing back the clam and taking a bite of bread.

"You mean things like E. Coli, Hepatitis, Red Tide?"

Josie shrugged.

"More for me."

The waitress arrived with our entrees; salmon for her, steak for me. I thanked the waitress, then attacked my steak. As always, it was perfect. I took a sip of wine then popped a Kalamata olive in my mouth. I chewed it slowly and glanced around the crowded lounge.

"Here we go again," I said, nodding toward the entrance to the bar.

Josie looked up from the salmon she was quickly devouring and frowned when she saw Jerry and Frederick scoping out the room. They both saw us at the same time, ignored us as if we were strangers, then continued to scan the lounge.

"How quickly they forget, huh?" Josie said, laughing.

"I think we hurt their feelings," I said, following their stare.

"Or their manhood."

"Now this is interesting," I said.

"What?" Josie said, following my eyes toward a table in the back corner of the lounge. "How about that? It looks like they made up."

I watched the two women as they leaned in close across the table. The whispered conversation was intense. I glanced back at Jerry and Frederick who continued to watch the two women at the table, then looked at each other and shook their heads. They turned and left the restaurant.

"I guess they didn't want to run the risk of being shot down twice in the same evening," Josie said, watching the two men leave.

"Yeah, probably," I said, still focused on the women in the corner of the lounge. "For two people who recently had a screaming match, they sure seem close at the moment."

"Maybe a lovers quarrel?"

"Anything's possible," I said.

Josie took another large bite of salmon and chewed in silence, deep in thought.

"Or it could be just the raw emotions brought on by shared grief," she said, finally. "You know, a recent death in the family."

"Except neither one is family. One was Crawford's girlfriend; the other worked for him."

"You know what I mean," Josie said.

"Yeah, but they certainly weren't exhibiting much grief when we saw them. It was more like open hostility."

"I'm sure their emotions are on overload," Josie said.

"Maybe," I said, pausing from my snooping long enough to take a bite of steak. "But why would they have been screaming at each other?"

"I don't know," Josie said, polishing off her last bite of salmon and looking down at her empty plate. "Well, I certainly made short work of that. I'm such a little piggy." She laughed at her joke and took a sip of wine. "Since they aren't family members, both of their situations are probably a bit shaky at the moment. And the ex-wife is arriving tomorrow. I can't imagine she's a big fan of the girlfriend. And if wifey is going to inherit the business, maybe Rosaline is nervous about losing her job."

"Maybe," I said, focusing on my dinner. I stared off into the distance.

"Uh, oh," Josie said.

"What?"

"You've got that look."

"What look?"

"The look you get when you think something's rotten, and you need to figure out what it is."

"I do not," I said. I caught the look Josie gave me, then shrugged. "Okay, maybe I do sometimes. But you said yourself that the whole thing seemed suspicious."

"Yes, I did. And I'm still having trouble getting past the maple syrup. But that doesn't mean somebody killed Crawford. Or that those two over there in the corner had anything to do with it."

"No, you're right. But wouldn't you like to be sure? I'm only thinking about Chloe's well-being."

Josie laughed loud enough to draw the attention of several people sitting nearby.

"You're unbelievable," she said.

"I couldn't live with myself if we ended up giving her back to a stone cold killer."

"A little dramatic, Suzy, even by your standards. Admit it, you just can't resist sticking your nose into something you consider a mystery."

"Aren't you curious?"

"Maybe a little," Josie said, wiping her mouth as she glanced back at the women in the corner. "Oh, this is interesting."

"What?" I said, turning my attention to the back of the lounge.

41

The two women had finished their intimate conversation and were now sitting back in their chairs and exchanging unpleasantries. I couldn't hear what they were saying above the noise, but it was clear that whatever truce they had agreed to was over.

"I wonder what set them off," I said.

"Could be anything," Josie said. "Wow, it's escalating."

"Yeah, it certainly is. And I doubt if it's about who's picking up the check."

We watched Roxanne stand and toss a full glass of red wine across the table. It hit Rosaline in the face and splattered her white blouse. Roxanne stormed out of the restaurant leaving the other woman at the table. Embarrassed, Rosaline calmly wiped her face with a napkin and did her best to clean her blouse while avoiding the stares she was getting. She tossed the napkin aside, then signed the check and got up from the table.

"C'mon," I said, grabbing a hundred dollar bill from my purse and tucking it under my plate.

"What are you doing?" Josie said, perusing the dessert menu.

"We're going to follow them."

"Follow them where?"

"How would I know where they're going?"

"But I wanted dessert."

"I'll buy you an ice cream later."

Josie reluctantly put the dessert menu down and got up from the table.

"Okay, so what's your plan?" she said, following me out of the lounge.

"We'll figure something out."

"Yeah, that oughta work," Josie said.

We waved goodbye to our waitress and headed for the front door.

"I hope they came in the same car," I said. "C'mon, I don't want to lose them."

"Okay, I'm coming, Miss Marples. Lead the way."

Chapter 8

We stood outside the restaurant and watched the two women wave their arms and point fingers at each other as they strode to their car. I couldn't make out what they were saying, but whatever it was, their conversation was heated. We waited until they got into their car, then Josie and I hopped into my SUV and waited.

"Now what?" Josie said, glancing at the women's car.

"Like I said, we'll follow them."

"They're staying on Candyland, so I think we already know where they're going."

"Maybe they have someplace else to go before they head back to the island."

"If the ice cream shop closes before we finish this nonsense, I'm not going to be happy," Josie said.

"Relax, we have ice cream back at the house."

"Mint chocolate chip?"

I thought about our ice cream inventory in the freezer.

"No, I don't think so."

Josie frowned and looked at her watch.

"We've only got about an hour before they close."

"Shhh," I said. "There they go."

We watched the car exit the parking area and turn left on Route 12, heading north. I pulled out and followed them at a safe distance.

"They don't seem to be in a hurry," I said.

"It's probably hard to drive and go ten rounds at the same time," Josie said.

"What on earth?" I said, glancing back through the rear view mirror.

"What is it?" Josie said, turning around in her seat.

"A car is coming up on us. Wow, it's flying. It just flashed its lights."

"Cop?"

"I don't think cop cars can go that fast," I said, slowing down to fifty and moving to the far right side of the two-lane highway.

The car flashed its lights one more time then blew by us as though we were parked. There was a quick tap of the horn, and I caught a glimpse of the wave the driver gave us.

"She is so going to jail," I said.

"Geez, that car is a rocket," Josie said. "What is it with your mom and fast cars?"

"I wish I knew. For someone who has no idea where she's going in life, she sure is in a hurry to get there."

"I think your mom knows exactly where she's going," Josie said, laughing.

"I guessing someplace very warm."

"You don't give her enough credit. I admire her ability to squeeze every last drop out of life."

"Yeah, maybe. I just wish she'd stop squeezing every drop out of me while doing it."

Josie laughed again and, as usual, it relaxed me. I refocused on the car in front of us. A few miles later, its right turn indicator started flashing.

"Interesting," I said. "Our new friends are turning away from the River, so we know they aren't heading for their boat."

The car turned off the highway, and I slowed down. I checked the rearview mirror and didn't see any other cars behind us. I slowed even more, turned off my headlights, and turned onto the small paved road.

45

"No lights?" Josie said. "It's nice to see your mom's not the only one in the family with a death wish."

"Relax," I said, peering through the windshield. "We're fine. Now, where the heck did they go?"

"I don't see any taillights."

"Me neither," I said, continuing to squint through the darkness. "Maybe they turned off somewhere."

"There you go. They disappeared," Josie said. "No sense wasting any more time. Can we get ice cream now?"

"Hang on," I said, coming to a stop and turning around. "Keep an eye out for side roads."

"At least turn the lights back on," Josie said.

I complied and drove slowly back towards the highway.

"There," Josie said, pointing out her window.

I pulled off the road onto a dirt road. I followed it for about two hundred yards, then stopped when we came to a single strand of thick chain draped about two feet off the ground across the road. It was locked and had a sign that read *Private Road* posted on both sides.

"Is it my imagination or is the chain still swinging back and forth?" I said.

"Could be the wind," Josie said.

"There's no wind tonight," I said. "They just went up that road."

"You know what that means, don't you?"

"That one of them had the key?"

"Yes. Or maybe both of them," I said. "What do you think?"

"About what?" Josie said, giving me a suspicious look.

"About going in. It can't be far. We can just walk it."

"In these shoes?" Josie said. "Not gonna happen. Besides, how would we explain ourselves if they happened to see us? Hi, guys. After the scene in

46

the restaurant, we thought we'd follow you and see what all the fighting was about?"

"You've got a point there," I said. "Okay, we'll come back another time."

"You mean as soon as possible."

"Why not?" I said, backing the car down the dirt road.

"You're unbelievable," Josie said. "Can we get ice cream now?"

"Sure."

"I want mint chocolate chip."

"So you said."

"And I want two scoops."

"Fine. Two scoops. Anything else?"

"I want sprinkles."

"Mint chocolate chip doesn't need sprinkles."

"Everything in life needs sprinkles," Josie said, leaning back in her seat and closing her eyes.

Chapter 9

Josie came in my office while I was doing some research on the Crawford Candy Company. She sat down and put her feet up on my desk and sipped her coffee.

"I found out what was bothering Sluggo," she said.

"Is he okay?" I said, looking up from the screen.

"He's fine," she said. "For the life of me, I couldn't figure out why he was so sluggish. So I took some X-rays."

"And?"

"He ate a football," she said, shaking her head. "One chunk of leather at a time."

"The whole thing?"

"Everything, including the laces."

"You didn't have to do surgery on him, did you?" I said, knowing that Jackson would be crushed if his beloved bulldog had to go through something like that while he was out of town.

"No, I decided it was a good chance for Sammy to get a real feel for some of the things we do around here. So I had him take the lead on giving Sluggo a high colonic."

"Yuck," I said, laughing. "How did Sammy handle it?"

"Not bad," Josie said, laughing. "Better than Sluggo. We might want to double up on Sluggo's walks today. He's still a bit... well, you know what I mean."

"Yeah, I got it," I said.

There was a knock on the door and Josie reached behind her to open it. Sammy stood in the doorway with a confused look on his face.

"Hey, Sammy," I said. "Josie was just telling me what a great job you did with Sluggo."

"I'd rather not talk about it," he said, cringing. "But there's something you need to see."

"What is it?" I said.

"It's Chloe."

I scrambled to my feet. "What's wrong?"

"Nothing's wrong," Sammy said. "I just don't know how I should handle it."

Josie and I followed him outside to the large fenced grass area we let the dogs play when the weather was good. We stood on the outside of the fence and watched the scene play out in front of us. Then Josie and I started laughing when we realized what was happening.

"Well, Australian Shepherds are bred to herd," Josie said.

I watched as Chloe continued to bark and force the other two dozen dogs into a loosely organized group. She was forcing them back toward the gate that led back inside the Inn. I called her, and when she heard my voice, she bolted toward me. I opened the gate, picked her up, then closed the gate and stroked her head.

"What a good girl," I said, still laughing.

"How does such a little dog do that?" Sammy said. "The Great Dane was scared to death of her."

"Tiny is scared of his own shadow," Josie said. "But I've seen Aussies herd thousands of sheep at one time."

"Cool," Sammy said. "You guys mind if I take my break now?"

"Sure, go ahead," I said, noticing the trail of dust rising in the distance.

Sammy pulled out his phone, attached ear plugs, and inserted them in his ears. He walked through the gate and began walking across the lawn while continuing to stare down at his phone.

49

"What's he doing?" Josie said, staring after him.

"Pokemon GO," I said, staring at the young man striding across the two-acre lawn, seemingly unaware of the dogs following him. "Maybe we should send Chloe after him."

"It might be nice to be young and oblivious again," Josie said, watching the Ferrari come tearing into the driveway throwing dirt and pebbles in all directions.

"Or old and oblivious," I said, shaking my head at my mother's driving.

I waved as she climbed out. She brushed her hair back, adjusted her sunglasses and stood next to the car. She gestured for us to come to her. I grumbled under my breath and headed her way like a sheepish schoolgirl. Josie followed with a huge smile on her face.

"I'm so glad my mother lives in Georgia," Josie said.

We approached the car, and my mother put her hands on her hips as she waited.

"Hello, darling. I just thought I'd swing by to see how your date went last night."

"If you must know, it was a complete waste of time. Where do you find these guys, Mom?"

"Who, Jerry? He's doing some work for me."

"I'm sorry to hear that, Mom. The guy is a total loser. With a capital L."

"Your standards are too high, darling. And I'd like you to give Jerry another chance. He's helping me out with some long-range financial planning, and I want him in a good mood while he's doing it."

"What's he going to be doing with your money, Mom?"

"Oh, he's just making sure everything is in order in case anything should happen."

50

She caught the stare I was giving her and laughed.

"Don't worry, darling. I'm not writing you out of the will."

"No, that's not what…never mind."

"Relax, dear. It's all related to tax implications and other money things I know you hate. But I would like you to consider another date with Jerry. He called me this morning and explained what happened."

"You mean about how you told him how Josie and I handle bad first dates?"

"Yes, well," she said, embarrassed. "I may have *overreached* a bit there. But as a favor to me, I wish you'd reconsider."

"I'll think about it, Mom."

"Good girl," she said, patting my arm. She glanced across the lawn. "Is that Sammy?"

"Yes," I said.

"How's he working out?"

"He's catching on quickly," Josie said. "He's a good kid."

"What on earth is he doing?" my mother said, removing her sunglasses to get a better look.

"At the moment, we think he's looking for Pokemon," I said.

"Well, I doubt if he's going to find him there," Josie said. "He's trudging right through the middle of the poo-pile."

Chapter 10

I stood on the front step and looked back out over the River. The property and the view that came with it were both magnificent. A seven hundred foot freighter was making its way through the main channel heading towards Lake Ontario about thirty miles upriver. Josie and I waited for the flag flying off the stern to come into view. We both saw the red and green flag emblazoned with a coat of arms at the same time.

"Portugal," we said simultaneously.

"Another saltie," I said. "That's the sixth one I've seen today."

For the unfamiliar, 'saltie' is the term we use to describe ships that cross the ocean as opposed to a 'laker' that travels the Seaway but remains on the River and Great Lakes throughout its journey. Seeing a seven hundred foot ship up close can be a bit disconcerting, especially when you consider they're navigating a tight shipping channel through dozens of granite islands and shoals that don't move no matter how hard you run into them, often at night, and sometimes through thick fog. But living here does provide the opportunity for one to become quite the flag expert.

"You think we're dressed right for this dinner?" Josie said, glancing down at her shorts and sandals.

"I guess," I said, checking out my outfit. It was similar to Josie's but, as always, she wore it better. "When in doubt, go island casual, right?"

Josie shrugged. "I guess. But these are money people. Maybe they take getting dressed for dinner more seriously than we do."

"We'll be fine. You ready?" I said.

Josie nodded and knocked on the front door. The door opened, and Carl the Gardener greeted us.

"Welcome, ladies," he said, gesturing for us to come in. "You both look great."

He must have psychic abilities since he never even glanced at me, much less at what I was wearing.

"Thanks," I said. "You doing double duty today?"

"I beg your pardon," he said.

"Aren't you the gardener?" I said.

"Oh, that," he said, chuckling. "That's just my day job. At night, I pretty much do anything they tell me to."

"And what did they tell you to do tonight?" I said.

"Join everyone for dinner, help Chef Claire out as necessary, assist with clean up. All the usual stuff. Oh, and try to keep everyone from killing each other."

He laughed, but I'm not sure he was joking. He led us into the library where we saw the girlfriend, Roxanne, and Rosaline sitting across from each other around a coffee table. They weren't at each other's throat, but they certainly weren't bosom buddies. They glanced up as we entered, then scowled at Carl.

"If you ladies will excuse me," Carl said. "I need to help out in the kitchen."

"Roxanne," Rosaline said, "Why don't you make yourself useful and get all of us a drink?"

Roxanne sighed loudly but got up and grabbed the empty glass Rosaline was holding up, then crossed to the other side of the library.

"Champagne, okay?" Roxanne said.

Josie and I nodded and sat down on the couch. Roxanne handed us our glasses, and we took a sip. It was delicious.

"I didn't get a chance the other day to tell you how sorry I am for your loss," I said to Rosaline.

53

"Yeah," she said, staring out a large picture window that overlooked the River. "It was tragic."

"The River can be a dangerous place," I said. "Especially at night."

"So everyone keeps telling me," Rosaline said.

She was already bored by the conversation. Or with me. Probably both.

"Do you spend much time on the River?" I said, glancing back and forth between the two women.

"As little as possible," Rosaline said. "I hate being surrounded by water. But Mr. Crawford loved spending time here, so you go where the work is, right?"

"How about you, Roxanne?" I said.

"Me?" she said, glancing up from her fresh manicure. "I just go where Bob tells me to go." Her voice caught, and her eyes welled with tears. "I mean where he told me to go."

It was the first sign of real emotion I'd seen from her. Or from anyone for that matter.

"So it was a boating accident, right?" I said.

Rosaline nodded slowly. "Yeah, he liked to take a boat out at night and just drift. And drink."

"We had some good nights out there," Roxanne said, taking a gulp of champagne.

"Yes, we know," Rosaline said. "When the wind was just right, everyone up and down the River could hear you."

"Don't be cruel," Roxanne said. "They were very special nights. At least they were until he got that stupid dog."

"Chloe?" I said, glancing at Josie.

"Oh, poor Roxanne," Rosaline said, laughing. "Replaced by a puppy."

"I was not replaced," Roxanne snapped. "It's just that he took the dog everywhere. It even slept in our bed. All I'm saying is that it cramped our style."

"Well, it's nice to see that you found a way to compensate," Rosaline said.

Roxanne whispered something under her breath that no one could understand. I doubt if it was a compliment.

"I'm sorry, ladies," Rosaline said, draining her glass. "You'll have to excuse, Roxanne. Mr. Crawford's demise has cast a rather dark shadow over her long-range plans."

"You're one to talk," Roxanne said.

"As I'm forced to remind you again, the difference between the two of us, Roxanne, is that I have an actual skill set to fall back on. The only thing you have to fall back on is…well, your back."

"I don't have to sit here and take this," Roxanne said, jumping to her feet.

"Sit," Rosaline snapped.

Now I understood why Rosaline seemed ambivalent to dogs. Given the way humans seemed to respond to her commands, dogs were probably irrelevant.

"Sit down, please. I'm sorry, Roxanne. I shouldn't have said that."

Roxanne sat down and wiped her eyes dry with a napkin. I glanced at Josie who was closely following the exchange.

"So Mr. Crawford took Chloe out on the River the other night?" I said, trying to change the subject. It came out awkward, and Rosaline gave me a strange look.

"Are you writing a book or something?" she said, glaring at me.

"No, nothing like that," I said, embarrassed. "It's just that it sounds like Mr. Crawford was very experienced with boats and the River."

"Accidents happen," Rosaline said, shrugging. "And who knows how much he'd had to drink."

"Was he a big fan of maple syrup?" Josie said.

Rosaline snorted and looked at Roxanne.

"Yeah, he loved the stuff," Roxanne said. "Drank it straight from the bottle."

"Hey, how did you know that?" Rosaline said, staring at Josie.

"It was all over the place when we found him," Josie said.

"What do you mean when you found him?" Rosaline said.

"We're the ones who found his body. You didn't know that?" I said.

"How on earth would I know that? I thought you two had just found the stupid dog."

Stupid dog? Maybe I should set her up with Jerry the Lawyer. They were perfect for each other.

"All the police said was that two fishermen found him," Rosaline said.

"That was us," Josie said. "And there was a big pool of maple syrup floating on the surface."

Rosaline stared at Josie, then glanced at Roxanne before responding. "Anything else?"

"What?" Josie said.

"Did you see anything else in the water?"

"You mean, apart from the dead body?" Josie deadpanned.

"Yes," Rosaline whispered, flushed with embarrassment.

"No," Josie said. "The body pretty much had my undivided attention."

I smiled but remained silent. I knew that Josie had decided to push the conversation a bit to see what sort of reaction she got. Under normal circumstances, she would never do anything to add to the suffering of a grieving family, but these people certainly weren't devastated. It was odd, but, apart from the uncertainty about their personal future with the Crawford family, they somehow seemed *relieved*.

"What else did you expect to be in the water?" Josie asked casually, glancing back and forth between the two women.

"Nothing," Rosaline said.

I glanced at Roxanne to gauge her reaction. She couldn't even maintain eye contact, so she settled for staring down at the floor.

"I guess it's not surprising," Josie said. "If he hit something or fell out of the boat when it was going fast, whatever you might expect to find near the body could have been thrown overboard."

"Or went down with the boat," Roxanne whispered.

"Sure," Josie said. "That's a distinct possibility."

"What kind of boat was it?" I said.

"What?" Rosaline said.

"The boat. Mr. Crawford had a lot of boats. Which one did he take out that night?"

Rosaline thought about it, then glanced at Roxanne who shrugged.

"I have no idea," Rosaline said.

"Which boat is missing?" I said.

"Again, I wouldn't have a clue. You'd have to ask Carl. He's the one who is supposed to keep track of things like that." She glanced at her watch and seemed relieved when she saw what time it was. "Time for dinner. Roxanne, why don't you take our guests into the dining room? I'll be along in a few minutes."

She got up and headed for the front door. I couldn't help but notice her removing her phone from the front pocket of her shorts as she stepped outside onto the porch.

Chapter 11

The dining room was massive as was the ornate wooden table that dominated the floor space. The table, capable of easily accommodating thirty people, was set for eight. I did the math and came up a couple of people short. Roxanne refilled our champagne glasses then plopped down wearily at one end of the table. She pointed at the chairs on either side of her, so Josie and I sat down across from each other and looked at each other. Josie shook her head as if to say, *It's your turn to talk,* so I turned to Roxanne.

"So, Roxanne," I said. "Did you grow up around here?"

"Nah," she said, taking a gulp of champagne. "I'm originally from L.A."

"Oh, California. Nice," I said.

"I guess," she said.

"How did you, uh, meet Mr. Crawford?" I said, doing my best to come across as casual without appearing nosy.

Truth be told, I was dying to know how she had hooked up with the dead candy magnate.

"He was the money guy behind one of my movies," she said, taking another gulp of champagne.

"Oh, you're an actress," I said. "Have you been in anything I might have seen?"

"I don't know," she said, looking up from her place setting long enough to glance at me. "You ever watch adult cable?"

"Adult cable? You mean adult as in not the Disney Channel?"

"Well, you certainly wouldn't see any of my movies on Disney," she said, laughing.

"Oh, I see." I felt my face flush with embarrassment.

"But they're of the softer variety. I refuse to do anything that could be called hardcore. I have my reputation as an actress to consider.

"Of course," I said.

"Completely understandable," Josie said, chiming in with a wink in my direction.

"So Mr. Crawford was your producer?"

"Yeah. At least he was until we started living together. Since then, my career has been on hiatus."

"And now?" I said.

"Now, I'm not sure," she said, getting up to refill her glass. Josie and I waved off her offer of more champagne, and she sat back down at the table. "It's going to come down to money. I don't want to go back into *acting*, but I don't have a lot of options. I'm not trained to do, well, anything."

I found myself feeling a touch of sympathy for her. I wasn't exactly sure why. It certainly wasn't the money question. She was wearing enough diamonds to fund a small war. Maybe it was because she seemed to have few options available to her. But, then again, she had made her own choices up to this point. She must have been satisfied with her role as the girlfriend, at least in the beginning.

Be careful what you wish for in life because you just might get it, right?

But before I had a chance to dig deeper into the source of my newfound empathy, the door leading into the dining room from the kitchen burst open, and an attractive woman in her fifties entered, followed closely by a very annoyed Rosaline.

"Great," Roxanne whispered, staring down at her lap.

"Let me guess," I whispered to her. "The ex-Mrs. Crawford."

"Who else?" Roxanne said.

Mrs. Crawford stopped near the fireplace, surveyed the table setting, glanced back and forth between Josie and me, then focused on Roxanne.

"Hello, Roxanne," she said, managing to scowl and smile at the same time.

It's a tough expression to pull off. I know this because it had taken my mother years to perfect it.

"Hi, Marge," Roxanne said, briefly making eye contact then staring back down into her lap.

"I almost didn't recognize you," Marge said. "What with you being in an upright position."

"Nice to see you, too, Marge," Roxanne said as she fumbled for her champagne glass.

Marge glared at Josie and me through narrowed eyes.

"Do I know you two?" Marge said.

"No, I'm Suzy," I said. "And this is Josie."

"Okay," she said, glancing back over her shoulder at Rosaline. "Explain their presence."

"They're the two women I mentioned over the phone. They were the ones who found Bob's body."

"I see," Marge said, continuing to take our measure.

"And they have some questions about what to do with Chloe. I invited them to dinner so they could discuss it with you."

"Chloe?" Marge said, frowning. "Who's that? Another of my ex-husband's playthings?"

"No, the dog," Rosaline said.

"Dog? He got a dog?" Marge said.

"Yes," I said. "A beautiful Australian Shepherd puppy."

"What happened, Roxanne? Were your scintillating conversational skills and cloying devotion enough to finally convince Bob about the fallacy of unconditional love between humans?"

"No, he was well versed in that long before we even started seeing each other. After all, he did learn at the foot of the master," Roxanne said.

"Oh, good one," I whispered to Roxanne.

Josie, mid-swallow, choked on her champagne, then wiped her mouth with a napkin. I looked down the table at Marge. She was fuming but apparently didn't have a good comeback. She sat down at the other end of the table and glared at Roxanne. Roxanne, already several glasses of champagne into her evening, was either oblivious to Marge's stare or had decided to ignore her.

"It's gonna be a long night," Josie whispered across the table.

I nodded, but before I could respond, the evening took an even weirder turn. The kitchen door opened partway, and a familiar face appeared in the opening.

"Here it is," the man said, entering. "I don't know how I ended up in the kitchen."

I nudged Josie's leg with my foot under the table. She glanced over her shoulder, then looked back at me confused.

"Hello, everyone," the man said. "I'm Jerry." He glanced around the table, then beamed when his eyes landed on mine. "Well, if it isn't my little Macadamia nut." He made a beeline for the empty chair on my left and plopped down.

"What are you doing here?" I said.

"I'm working," Jerry said, helping himself to a glass of champagne. "What's your excuse?"

"I'm trying to find a good home for a puppy," I said.

"Noble work," he said, then took a gulp of champagne.

61

"What are you working on?" I said.

"Her," he said, nodding at Marge. "Trying to get her finances in order now that, well, you know. Dead husband and all."

"Dead ex-husband," Josie said.

"Right," Jerry said, leering at Josie. "You look fantastic tonight."

The kitchen door opened, and George, the harried older man we'd met briefly during our first visit entered. He glanced around the seating pattern and glared at us, obviously annoyed that all the seats at our end of the table were taken. He sat down next to Rosaline and Marge.

"Okay, now that we're all here," Marge said. "We can eat." She picked up a small dinner bell and rang it.

"A dinner bell?" Josie whispered. "The kitchen's eight feet away."

I laughed and got a glare from Marge. Apparently, silence-breaking laughter at the dinner table was a no-no.

Carl, trailed by a woman in chef attire, entered carrying trays with steaming soup.

"Great," Josie said. "I'm starved."

I nodded and tried to remain patient. I was also starving, and I love soup.

"So, Chef Claire," Marge said. "What are we having for our first course?"

"I thought I'd stay local in honor of Mr. Crawford. This soup was his favorite."

"Yuk," Roxanne whispered.

I glanced at her, then focused back on the chef.

"This is walleye chowder. You'll notice a touch of fennel and sherry that both soften and accent the flavor of the fish. Enjoy."

With that, the chef headed back to the kitchen. Carl finished serving everyone then sat down next to Rosaline. I couldn't miss the glare he was getting from Roxanne.

"Great. Fish soup," I whispered.

"I hate this soup," Roxanne said.

Josie chuckled as she attacked her bowl. I stared down at mine and toyed at it with my spoon.

"So, Jerry," Marge said. "Did you have any luck tracking that information down?"

"Uh, no, not yet, Mrs. Crawford," Jerry said. "I'll get right back on it after dinner."

"Track what down?" Rosaline said.

"Nothing that concerns you, Rosaline," Marge said, waving her question off with the back of her hand.

"If it deals with the company, I'm afraid that it does concern me," Rosaline said.

"Maybe it did two days ago, my dear," Marge said, doing the scowl-smile thing again.

Man, she was really good at it. My mother could learn a few tricks from her.

"What does that mean?" Rosaline said, putting her spoon down and wiping her mouth.

"It means that two days ago, you worked for my ex-husband. Now you work for me. At least you do for the moment."

"Work for you? Based on what?" Rosaline said.

"His will. What do you think I'm basing it on?" Marge said.

"He changed his will after your divorce," Rosaline said. "At least that's what he told me."

"Bob told people a lot of things," Marge said. "He was very good at telling people what they wanted to hear. Isn't that right, Roxanne?"

Roxanne, torn between responding or taking a mouthful of soup, chose the latter. She gagged a spoonful down. I admired her courage.

"Have you seen this so-called new will?" Marge said, refocusing her attention on Rosaline.

"No, not yet," Rosaline said. "Bob said it was locked away for safe keeping."

"I see," Marge said, then glanced quickly at Jerry.

Jerry gave her the smallest of nods in return, but I caught it. I looked at Josie. She'd also seen it. Roxanne missed it since she was still gagging into her napkin. I noticed Josie had finished her bowl of the dreaded chowder and slowly slid mine across the table and pulled back her empty one. She shook her head at me, then started working on the fresh bowl.

I sat quietly, doing my best to fend off Jerry's flirtations as I listened to my stomach rumble. I studied Marge and Rosaline at the other end of the table. They chatted sporadically, but it was obvious that they shared a mutual contempt. Across the table from Rosaline, George, the harried one, ate with the expression of a man on death row.

It had to be the fish chowder.

Perhaps, now that Marge had arrived, from a career perspective, he was about to be a dead man. I knew they were all trying to deal with the death of a man who had been a major player in their lives, but there was no sense of any *shared* grief. As I watched, I was even more convinced that the candy magnate Crawford had been the victim of something other than an accidental drowning.

Before I could dwell on my theory, the chef entered pushing a cart stacked with covered dishes. I leaned forward in anticipation, hoping for a

64

steak, or perhaps pork tenderloin. I was so hungry I would have settled for a peanut butter sandwich. Then I sat back as I picked up the scent.

"Ugh," I whispered.

"What?" Josie said, finishing the last of my chowder.

I nodded at the cart.

"Salmon."

"Yum," Josie said, chuckling. "I guess it's not your night."

Carl helped clear the table while the chef placed our entrees in front of us. I stared down at the golden piece of grilled salmon and listened to the ooohs and ahhs coming from Jerry and Josie. Even Roxanne was digging in with gusto.

Traitor.

I sat staring at my piece of salmon, then squirted lemon all over it and poked at it with my fork. Then I gave up and nudged Josie under the table with my foot. She looked up from her plate and nodded when I indicated that she should help herself to mine. I excused myself from the table and headed for the kitchen.

Chapter 12

I entered the massive kitchen and found it empty. I don't know why I expected to see a bunch of kitchen staff bustling around. After all, there were only eight of us at the dinner table. Maybe it was because the kitchen reminded me of one you'd find in a restaurant. Maybe it was because of my perceptions about how the rich lived their lives, surrounded by a large collection of people there to do their bidding. Maybe it was because I hadn't eaten since breakfast and my blood sugars had dropped to dangerous levels, reducing me to a babbling idiot.

Then I smelled it. Immediately on point, I glanced around the kitchen for the source. Just as I spied the oven in question, the chef entered the kitchen drying her hands on a towel. She jumped back when she saw me, and it took her a moment to catch her breath. Then she smiled at me. It was the first genuine smile I'd gotten from anyone on the island.

"Wow, you startled me," she said. "I'm Chef Claire. Can I help you?"

"I sure hope so," I said, sniffing the air.

"I'm sorry," she said. "Did I forget to bring something to the table? Perhaps you need some more lemon for your fish?"

"Uh, no," I said. "Please don't take offense, but I hate fish. And when I use that term, I'm talking about an *intense* hatred."

Instead of being offended, she laughed.

"I don't like it either. But it was Mr. Crawford's favorite. And since tonight's dinner was supposed to be in his honor, I thought I should at least try to do my part."

"Was supposed to be in his honor?" I said, doing my best not to come across as too suspicious.

"Yeah."

"And it isn't?"

"You've been sitting at the table. Does it seem like a fond farewell to you?"

"Uh, no," I said. "It seems like a major annoyance for all of them. Sorry to change the subject, but am I smelling bacon?"

"That's my dinner," Chef Claire said, heading to the oven. She opened it, and the smell was overpowering. "Bacon wrapped chili dogs. Care to join me?"

I must have been spending way too much time with my dogs because my knees buckled, my tongue dropped, and I think I started drooling. Just call me Pavlov. I wiped my mouth with the back of my hand and nodded.

"If you have enough," I whispered as I stared at the six hot dogs lovingly wrapped with thick slices of bacon.

"We have plenty," she said, removing a tray of freshly baked rolls from another section of the oven. "I always make more than I can eat in one sitting. But then I have to hide the leftovers if I expect them to be here when I'm looking for a late night snack."

She cut open one of the hot rolls, slathered it with mustard, then placed one of the bacon wrapped dogs on top, and carefully covered it with a generous portion of chili.

"You want to start with one?" Chef Claire said.

"If I have to," I whispered.

"What?"

"Nothing," I said, staring at the steaming object of my desire in her hand. "One's fine."

"How about two?" she said, laughing.

"You read my mind," I said.

Chef Claire gestured at a large granite island surrounded by high-backed leather stools, and I took a seat. She placed the plate in front of me, then headed for the fridge. When she opened the door, I saw the inside shelves lined with bottles of maple syrup. She returned with bowls of potato salad and cole slaw. I waited until she joined me, then attacked one of the chili dogs. I murmured with delight, took a second bite, and sighed.

"Good, huh?" Chef Claire said, quickly working her way through her first dog.

"Best I've ever had," I said, taking a moment to wipe my mouth before diving into the potato salad.

"This used to be my signature dish," she said, suddenly starting off into the distance.

"Used to be?"

"Well, I guess it still is in some ways. But when I had my food truck, this was the thing people always wanted."

"You had a food truck? Where was that?"

"Los Angeles. That was where I met Bob. Mr. Crawford. Or as he used to say, that was where he discovered me. One day, he and Roxanne had one of these, and an hour later I was under contract as his personal chef."

"Impressive," I said. "Mr. Crawford made you an offer you couldn't refuse, right?"

Chef Claire laughed, then started working on her second chili dog.

"Yeah, I was doing well with the food truck, but when he said he'd double whatever I was making... well, you know the drill."

"So, you two were close," I said.

"At first, yes. Then Bob decided we should get *really* close."

"Ah, I got it," I said, studying her closely. "How did Mr. Crawford handle rejection?"

"Not well," she said, taking a sip of water. "But as you can see, I have access to an impressive knife collection."

I laughed, then stopped when I realized I wasn't sure if she was joking.

"And I guess that wouldn't have gone over well with Roxanne, either."

"Roxanne? That little golddigger is the least of my worries."

"She does seem pretty harmless," I said, staring at the two remaining chili dogs.

"Maybe. Maybe not. Did Roxanne tell you her story?" Chef said, reading my mind and grabbing the remaining two chili dogs from the stovetop. She handed me one and set the other on her plate. Since I was one dog ahead of her, I thought about slowing down, but then changed my mind.

"You mean the story about how she met Mr. Crawford when he was producing one of her films?" I said, grabbing a chunk of chili that was trying to escape.

"She met him when she was turning tricks outside my food truck," Chef said, staring at me.

"Really?"

"She left that part out, huh? What a surprise."

"She was a hooker?"

"Yeah, she was always hanging around at lunchtime. A lot of successful people ate at my food truck. I couldn't get rid of her. I ended up calling the cops several times, but she always found a way to stay out of trouble."

"Found a way?"

"Think about it," Chef said, piling coleslaw on her plate. "I'm pretty sure Bob was about to cut her loose."

"Really, why?"

69

"I'm not sure. After I turned him down, Bob didn't share much with me. My guess is that it was one part boredom, one part the fatigue of dealing with Roxanne's extracurricular activities."

"I see," I said, finally slowing down my intake of food. "So what's the deal with the ex-wife?"

"Marge the Malevolent? What you see is what you get. There's no mystery there. I'm sure she showed up just to make sure Rosaline and Roxanne don't try to screw her out of what she thinks is still hers."

"You mean the company?"

"All of it," Chef Claire said, pushing her plate away. "Whew, I'm full."

"But they are divorced, right?"

"Well, that's where it gets interesting. Apparently, as rumor has it, Marge signed the divorce papers, but she never got a copy back with Mr. Crawford's signature on it. If that's true, all bets are off regarding who gets what."

"And what's going to happen to those who end up getting nothing."

"You're a smart woman," Chef Claire said, grabbing both our plates and setting them in the sink. "I've been meaning to ask you, how's Chloe doing?"

"She's great," I said. "You know, you're the first person here who has asked about her."

"Does that surprise you? She's a great dog. Bob never went anywhere without her."

"She's amazing."

"You need to make sure you get to keep her. This isn't a good place for her to be now that Bob's gone."

I nodded. My sentiments exactly.

"So what about you?"

"Me? Well, Marge did offer me a position as Executive Chef at one of their resort properties in the Bahamas."

"That sounds pretty good," I said.

"Yeah, I'll probably take it. I need to get out of here while the getting is good. No more daily interactions with the Crawfords and their minions." Then she laughed. "And no more dealing with his endless love for fish."

"Or maple syrup," I said, unable to resist testing the water.

Her eyes narrowed, and she stared at me before forcing a smile.

"That's right," she said, turning to the sink. "You were the one who found him in the water."

"He loved his maple syrup, right?"

"Yeah," she said, her back still turned to me. "Too much. And it just might have been his undoing."

Great. That's all I needed. Another suspect. I wondered about what her motive could have been. Forced to cook and eat fish on a daily basis would have been enough for me, but I doubted if that had been enough to turn Chef Claire into a killer.

"Thanks again for dinner," I said to her back. "You're a lifesaver."

"I've never been called that before. But you're welcome."

Chapter 13

I went back into the dining room and discovered it empty. Hearing noise coming from the front porch, I walked outside and found everyone eating cake and ice cream. I sat down next to Josie and watched as she shoveled the dessert into her mouth.

"How on earth do you continue to eat the way you do and not gain a pound?" I said.

"I am blessed with an exceptionally high metabolism rate," she said, pausing to take a sip of coffee. "You want some?"

"No, I'm full."

Josie raised an eyebrow at me. "On what?"

"Bacon chili dogs," I said.

"How many?"

"Only three," I said, gently rubbing my stomach.

"You're one to talk," Josie said, polishing off the last bite of cake.

"What did I miss?"

She wiped her mouth with a napkin and pushed the empty plate away.

"Nothing much. And all of it confirms what we've been thinking. They all seem to hate each other. But for different reasons. And the only thing they have in common is their complete lack of sympathy for the recently departed Mr. Crawford."

"Even Roxanne?"

"Yeah, even her. I get the impression that Crawford had either just dumped her, or was about to."

"Well, Chef Claire certainly isn't a fan of her."

"Really? Do tell," Josie said.

I glanced around the porch and decided the rest of the conversation should wait until we were alone.

"Later," I said. "Did Jerry behave himself at the table?"

"I guess," she said. "He made a few comments that I ignored. Then he focused most of his attention on Roxanne. I caught them sharing a few looks that seemed to linger."

"They lingered?"

"Yeah, big time lingering."

"Interesting," I said.

"Not really. But Rosaline sure didn't like it," Josie said. "But it was all pretty pedestrian. They were the basic, *your place or mine* kind of thing."

"I hope he brought his checkbook."

"What?"

"Nothing."

"Are you ready to get out of here? I need to work off this meal, and I think the walk down to the boathouse just might do it."

"Sounds good," I said, glancing down the porch. "Let's go say our goodbyes."

We got up and approached Marge who was sitting by herself staring out at the River.

"I'd like to thank you for dinner, Mrs. Crawford," I said.

"What?" she said, coming out of her trance. "Oh, yeah, you two. Sure, whatever. You're welcome."

"I just need to ask you one question. It's about Chloe."

"Who?"

"Chloe. Mr. Crawford's dog."

"What about it?" she said.

I took a deep breath and swallowed hard before asking the question.

"Do you want her?"

To my delight, she laughed long and hard.

"Me? What on earth would I do with a dog?"

"Probably ruin it," Josie whispered.

I reached back and gently smacked her on the arm to shut up. Marge either hadn't heard Josie or had chosen to ignore the comment.

"So you don't mind if I keep her? I mean, she's gotten pretty settled into her new surroundings, and I'd hate to disrupt her lifestyle again. She's been through a lot lately."

"Disrupt her *lifestyle?*"

"Well, you know what I mean," I said, for some reason flushed with embarrassment by my choice of words.

"Keep it," she said, dismissing me with a wave of her hand. "I have more than enough to deal with at the moment. Besides, the only thing I'd do with it would be to change its name to Bob and scream at it all day."

For some reason, she found that idea funny.

"Get off the couch, Bob. How many times do I have to tell not to pee on the rug, Bob? Roll over and play dead, Bob. Yeah, that's it, Bob. Play dead. Good boy."

She continued to laugh. I glanced back at Josie, who nodded at the boathouse. We waved goodbye to the others and started making our way down the long set of stone steps.

"Weird," Josie said.

"Weird's a word for it," I said, fighting back a touch of chili dog heartburn. "I think the only grief any of them are feeling is the fact that he didn't go a lot sooner."

"You got any primary suspects in mind?" Josie said.

"Yeah, I've got a list," I said. "You?"

"I've got three," Josie said.

We reached the boathouse, and I slowly climbed into the boat and started the engine. Josie untied the lines and hopped into the boat with a thud.

"Wow," she said. "I ate too much."

"You always eat too much," I said, backing the boat away from the dock. "What you don't do is ever gain any weight."

"Well, if I have to keep eating your dinner to cover for you, that's going to change," she said, climbing into the seat next to me.

I turned the lights on, but the moonless night was very dark.

"I think we should head for deep water and just take the long way home," I said, heading for the main channel.

"Good idea," Josie said. "You know, now that I'm out here in complete darkness, I can see how Crawford could have just had an accident."

"Yes, he could have," I said, pulling on my jacket.

"But you don't think he did, do you?" Josie said.

"No," I said, shaking my head. "Do you?"

"Not a chance."

"So who's on your list of suspects?" I said, feeling a rush of adrenaline.

"Well, number one for me is Roxanne?" Josie said.

"Really?"

"Yeah, she has a lot to lose. At least from her perspective."

"I can see that," I said, squinting through the darkness. "And the last thing Roxanne wants is to have to go back to her old career."

"Actress?"

"Hooker."

"Really?"

"Yup."

"Says who?"

"Chef Claire."

75

"How does she know that ?"

"Prior history," I said. "She says that's how Roxanne first met Crawford in LA."

"So Roxanne lied to us?"

"Yeah, but that doesn't necessarily mean she killed him," I said. "If I was a hooker, I don't think I'd be telling a couple of strangers about it."

"You? A hooker?"

I laughed at the idea.

"Imagine that."

"I'm trying," Josie said, laughing along. "The way your love life is going these days, you're having a hard enough time giving it away."

"Hey, I'm just extremely selective," I said. "You should talk. You're worse than I am."

"So I'm picky," Josie said. "Who's on your list?"

"Roxanne's on the list, but she's not my number one. I'm thinking the ex-wife."

"Marge? But she wasn't even in town when it happened."

"Or so she says," I said, slowing down. "Great. The fog's rolling in."

"Just go slow," Josie said, glancing out over the water. "I hate being out here when it's foggy."

"Me too. Chef Claire told me an interesting tidbit about a rumor that the divorce was never finalized. At least from a legal perspective."

"Well, that would certainly change things," Josie said, tearing open a Snickers.

"Really?" I said, staring at the candy bar.

"What can I say? Fog always makes me hungry. You want a bite?"

I shook my head and refocused on the bank of fog forming on top of the water.

"Our Chef Claire is certainly a fountain of information," Josie said through a mouthful of chocolate.

"Yes, she is. And that's one of the reasons she's on my list."

"Interesting. Do tell."

"It was just the way she reacted to parts of our conversation. And she and Crawford had some history."

"Horizontal history?"

"She says no," I said.

"You believe her?"

"I don't know yet. But she did have some good things to say about Chloe, so she's earned the benefit of the doubt for the moment."

Josie nodded and continued to make short work of the candy bar.

"So how were the chili dogs?"

"Fantastic. I doubt if we'll be able to recreate them, but it's worth a shot. Who else is on your list?"

"I have the ex-wife as well. And my third one is Rosaline."

"Me too," I said. "Why do you think she might have done it?"

"It has to be something to do with her role in the company. She's so corporate."

"Yeah, something about her bugs me."

"Stepford wife syndrome," Josie said, crumpling the candy wrapper and sliding it into her pocket.

"Exactly. Do companies train them to have that dead-eyed expression or are they recruited like that?"

"Probably a lot of both," Josie said. "And what was that snippet of conversation at the dinner table about a new will? Things got weird in a hurry when that came up."

"I know. That was strange. And when Chef Claire mentioned the rumor about the divorce not being finalized, that was when I put Marge on the top

77

of my list. If she is still legally married to Crawford, the last thing she'd want surfacing is a new will."

"Makes sense," Josie said. "Say, you don't think Jerry the Lawyer could be working some scheme with her, do you?"

"Hmm, I hadn't until now," I said, rolling the idea around in my head. "Should we put him on the list?"

"Probably couldn't hurt," Josie said. "But you're the one who's going to have to keep an eye on him. He creeps me out."

"Great," I said, frowning. "Don't forget, we still need to follow up on the house behind the chain."

"Yeah," Josie said. "But not tonight. I'm stuffed."

"So you keep saying. If more than one person is involved, it opens up a whole range of possible partners in crime."

"Based on what we saw at Tondeuse, we already have Roxanne and Rosaline as a possibility."

"I don't see them working together, but you never know."

"Marge and Rosaline."

"Maybe," I said. "Assuming there's some connection to the business we don't know about."

"Chef Claire?" Josie said.

"Absolutely. And she could be working with any of the others. But Chef Claire seems to be the type who'd go solo."

"Carl?" Josie said.

"The gardener? Now that is a brilliant insight."

"Thanks," Josie said, then frowned. "Why?"

"Because he controls the boats. And he's the perfect choice to use for a cover story about who was or wasn't using one of the boats that night."

"I guess it was a brilliant insight, wasn't it?" Josie said, laughing.

"And now that I think about it," I said, slowing the boat even more. "If Crawford died in a boating accident and since the boat wasn't recovered, why isn't there an empty slip in the boathouse."

"There isn't?" Josie said.

"No, that's why we had to park at the dock."

"Now that is interesting. So Carl goes on the list."

"He sure does," I said. "And somewhere near the top until we know more."

"Carl could be working with any number of people," Josie said.

"He certainly could. There's Marge, Rosaline, Roxanne, Chef Claire, and who knows who else might be out there."

"I'll grab a copy of the phone book," Josie said, laughing. "Assuming they're still making phone books."

"What are you babbling about?"

"Suzy, we've been on the boat for about fifteen minutes, and our list of suspects has almost doubled."

"I guess we're just keeping our options open," I said, shrugging.

"Either that or we're not very good at this sort of thing."

We both started laughing loudly. In fact, we were laughing so loud we almost didn't hear the roar of a powerful boat approaching us from behind. I glanced back through the darkness trying to see through the fog as it drew closer, then pushed the throttle to full and turned the boat left toward shallow water. The massive boat, running without lights, roared past us on the starboard side, scraped the side of our boat and drenched us with its wake. When I was sure the boat wasn't coming back, I slowed down, and we drifted, enveloped by a dense patch of fog near the shore.

"Wow," I said, fighting to catch my breath. "That was close."

"And not accidental," Josie said.

"Definitely not. I think we touched a nerve with someone tonight."

"Yeah. You think they were going for the kill shot or just sending us a message?"

"I don't know. Does it matter?"

"No," Josie said, shaking her head. At least I think she was shaking her head. The fog was that thick.

"Let's get off the River and go home."

"Good idea," Josie said.

"You want to stop for ice cream?"

"No, thanks," Josie said. "I think I just lost my appetite."

Chapter 14

It was one of those mornings that made you feel glad to be alive. The River was a massive sheet of blue glass as the sun worked its way through the pines. I rubbed the sleeping Chloe's ears and sipped my coffee as I watched the early morning activities of our neighbors. Mr. Allison was about to head out for some fishing with his grandson. Mrs. Jones, a retired teacher, was already working in the garden. Her tomato plants were off to a great start, and I knew it wouldn't be long before she showed up with the annual basket of canned vegetables and sauces she gave all her friends and neighbors. I returned her wave and Chloe, stretched out across my lap, opened one eye and gave me the *why'd you stop* look.

"Sorry, but I needed that hand to wave," I said. "The other one is reserved for my coffee." Chloe seemed satisfied with my explanation and went back to sleep as soon as I resumed rubbing her ears.

Yes, it was a good day to be alive. But given how close Josie and I had come to getting killed last night, I could be sitting outside in the middle of a frigid blizzard, and it would still be one of days.

Josie, dressed in her scrubs, stepped outside and sat down in the Adirondack chair next to me.

"You're getting an early start," I said.

"Yeah, I have a surgery scheduled for eight-thirty. And I have a bunch of paperwork waiting for me. If we're going to play detective tonight, I won't be able to get to it later."

"Are you okay?"

"Yeah, I guess," she said, waving to Mrs. Jones. "But I'm still a bit rattled. We were very close to being fish food."

"I know," I said, squirming further back into my chair as Chloe made more room for herself on my lap.

Josie watched and laughed as Chloe ended up with most of the chair. "She's already getting too big for your lap."

"Try telling her that," I said, managing to pick up my coffee. "I thought we'd head out just after dark."

"Sounds good," Josie said as she turned her head at a noise coming from inside the house.

"Hellooooo!"

"Great," I said. "We're out here, Mom."

My mother peered through the screen door and stepped outside onto the porch.

"Good morning," she said, crossing in front of us and standing with her back against the railing as she studied both of us.

"You're up early," I said. "You want coffee?"

"No, I'm good, darling," she said, staring at Chloe. "Have you managed to finalize the adoption proceedings?"

"Yes," I said. "We closed the deal last night. We had dinner at Candyland Island."

"Beautiful place," she said. "How did that go?" She glanced back and forth at Josie and me.

I caught Josie's eye and gave her a slight shake of my head.

"It had its moments," Josie said.

"And we ran into Jerry, your financial advisor," I said.

"Really? What on earth was he doing there?"

"Apparently, he's helping Marge Crawford out."

"Interesting," she said, then shifted gears. "Well, I just stopped by to see if you're free and would like to join me today."

"Where are you going?"

"Shopping."

"You know I'm not much for shopping, Mom."

"I'm going to Montreal."

Oooh, Montreal. One of my favorite places. And I have a good friend from Montreal I haven't seen in a long time. It was definitely a tempting offer.

"What do you say, darling? We'll put the Ferrari through its paces, do some great shopping, maybe catch an early dinner at Europea, and I can work on my French."

"Your French is terrible, Mom."

"Hence, my invitation for you to join me," she said, beaming at me.

I looked at Josie. "Ma mère ne sait même pas quand elle est d'être insultant."

"Je me suis toujours pensé qu'il était l'un de ses meilleures qualités," Josie said, laughing.

"What are you two talking about?" my mother said. "Speak English."

"Yeah, you're going to work on your French," I said, finishing my coffee.

"So what do you say, darling? Feel like spending the day together? I'm buying."

"I would, Mom. But I'm buried with work today."

"Spoilsport," she said in mock indignation. "Okay, it's your loss. Is there anything you need?"

"No," I said. "I think I'm good."

"Really? That ratty bathrobe could certainly use an upgrade."

"My bathrobe is fine, Mom."

"If you say so, darling," she said. "Have you given any more thought to a second date with Jerry?"

Wow. I didn't see that one coming. That's the thing about having a conversation with my mother. Just when you think you've survived, she does a one-eighty and throws you a curve.

"Yes, I have," I said, glancing at Josie. "I'm considering it."

"That's wonderful," she said. "I'll set something up and let you know. Leave everything to me."

"Geez, Mom."

She waved off my protest and headed for the door.

"I have to run. You sure you don't want me to pick up something nice for you?"

"No, I'm good, Mom. But thanks."

"Okay. How about you, Josie?"

"No, Mrs. C. I can't think of anything I need."

"You two," she said, shaking her head. "Always worrying about what you need. It is okay occasionally to get something just because you want it."

"I'll try to remember that, Mom. Drive carefully. By that, I mean try to keep it under a hundred."

She laughed and departed with a wave. Josie started walking down the hill to the Inn. I headed inside, gave Chloe her morning snack, then showered and got ready for work.

Chapter 15

I parked on the side of the road, turned the headlights off but left the car running. I switched on the overhead light and looked at Josie in the passenger seat.

"You ready?" I said, pulling the strap attached to my binoculars over my head.

"I guess," Josie said. "You want to run the plan by me one more time?"

"It's simple," I said. "We'll just climb over the gate and follow the road. There has to be a house back there, right?"

"There's only one way to find out," Josie said, opening her door.

I turned the car off, climbed out, and locked it. My phone rang. I considered letting it go to voice mail but checked the number.

"My mother," I said to Josie. I leaned against the car, put the phone on speaker, and answered the call. "Hi, Mom. How was Montreal?"

"I'm still here, darling."

"Really? Did some charming French Canadian man make you an offer you couldn't refuse?"

"Well, I wouldn't necessarily consider him charming, but he did make me an offer I couldn't refuse."

"I'm going to need some clarification, Mom."

"The man who made the offer was a cop. I'm in jail."

"What?" I said, shaking my head at Josie. "What on earth did you do?"

"Apparently, 110 in a 60. The cop said I almost broke his radar gun."

"Geez, Mom. What is wrong with you?"

"Don't start, darling. I'm having a very bad evening."

"Okay, what do you need?"

"I need to make bail. And the police won't accept any of my credit cards. I think they're being particularly snotty about the whole thing, but they're holding all the cards. Literally. They confiscated all my credit cards. I feel completely violated. They even had the audacity to take the new Gucci bag I just bought."

"Yeah, cops are funny about things like that."

"I repeat. Don't start."

"What do you need?"

"I need you to drive up here and bail me out."

"Nice try, Mom," I said. "Not gonna happen. What else do you need?"

"Five thousand dollars."

"Okay," I said. "Let me call my friend. Her name's Marie. I'm sure she'll help you out. Just remember to pay her back."

I unlocked the car, grabbed a pen and jotted the address of the jail down on my hand.

"Okay, Mom. I'll call her. Hopefully, she's in town. I'll give her your number as well. Hang in there."

"Thank you, darling."

"Hey, Mom," I said, suddenly confused. "How come he didn't just give you a speeding ticket?"

"Well, I thought it would be a good time to try working some French into our conversation. You know, maybe he would take pity on me and go easy."

"Oh, no," I said. "What did you say to him?"

"I told him I thought he was a wonderful policeman."

"No, how did you say it in French?"

"Let's see. I said, *Je pense que vous êtes un cochon sale.*"

Josie and I laughed.

"Mom, you told him you thought he was a filthy pig."

86

"I did? Oh, my. Then I guess I can see why he got so mad. I think I better apologize to him."

"Yes, that would be a good start, Mom. But do it in English."

"Funny, darling. Go make your phone call, please."

"Hang tight, Mom."

"Thanks, darling. I'll swing by in the morning and tell you all about it," she said, hanging up.

"She's indestructible," Josie said.

"Yeah, she'll probably end up with the phone number of the cop who arrested her."

I called my friend Marie, explained the situation, and she agreed to take care of my mother's bail. We spent a few minutes catching up, pledged to get together soon, then I hung up. I turned my phone off, and Josie and I started walking up the hill that led to the chainlink gate.

"My mother, the criminal," I said, shaking my head.

"She needs to rethink the Ferrari," Josie said.

"Yeah, she needs to get something a bit safer. Like a tank."

I turned on the flashlight as we neared the gate. We stepped over the chain that stretched across the road, and I turned the flashlight off. We headed up the dirt road in complete darkness.

"Spooky," Josie said.

"Yes, but the flashlight is too bright to leave on. I don't think it's a good idea to announce our arrival."

"Okay, lead the way."

We continued up the road for several hundred feet. The only sound was our feet shuffling over the dirt and stone driveway. We saw a house with several lights on and two cars parked in front. Next to the house was another structure. I tried to make it out through the dim light.

"What is that? A garage?" I said, coming to a stop on the side of the road near a strand of pine trees.

"No, it's not a garage," Josie said. "It looks like a greenhouse."

"Makes sense," I said. "A lot of people try to extend the growing season."

"Yeah," Josie said. "How do you want to play it?"

"Let's head to the other side and get a little closer. From there we should be able to see through the front window."

Josie nodded and followed me across the road. We slowly made our way to another strand of trees about a hundred feet from the house. We both raised our binoculars and scanned the house.

"See anything?" Josie said.

"Only about a thousand mosquitos," I said, slapping at my arm. "I knew I forgot something."

"Bug spray would have been nice," she said, also slapping herself. "Let's get this over with."

I peered through the binoculars at the car parked outside the house.

"Do you recognize either of the cars?"

"No," she said, staring through her binoculars. "Here we go. Now this is interesting."

"What?" I said, trying to follow her line of sight.

"Downstairs. Second light on the right."

"Is that Carl the Gardener?" I said.

"It certainly is," Josie said.

"I guess I just assumed that he lived on the island. You think this is his house?"

"Well, if the greenhouse is any clue, that would be my guess."

"Then I wonder what Roxanne and Rosaline were doing visiting him late at night," I said.

"That is a good question," Josie said. "Another one would be who is visiting him tonight."

I continued staring at the house through the binoculars. I scanned the kitchen and caught a glimpse of movement.

"Kitchen. Last light on the left. Chef Claire appears to be cooking dinner," I said, lowering my binoculars.

"Can you tell what she's making?" Josie said.

I stared at her.

"Really? That's your question?" I said. "What's she making for dinner?"

"Never mind. It's not important. What do you know? Carl and Chef Claire?" she said. "I didn't see that one coming."

"What possible motive could they have to kill Crawford?"

"No, I wasn't talking about that. I meant I didn't see the possibility of those two dating."

"Well, we don't know if that's what is going on. They work together. Maybe they're just friends," I said.

We both focused our binoculars back on Carl who was stretched out on the couch in the living room staring intensely at something inside the house.

"He's watching TV," Josie said.

"Yeah," I said, then saw Chef Claire enter the room and climb on top of Carl and kiss him hard. "Then again, maybe they're *really good* friends."

Josie chuckled.

"Okay, kids," she said, staring through her binoculars. "Time to come up for air."

"So we know that Carl is getting busy with at least one of the women from the island."

"And maybe two, or even three of them."

89

"Yeah," I said. "Let's go take a closer look while they're preoccupied. I'd like to get a look at the greenhouse."

"Good idea," Josie said, following me down the road that led to the house.

We approached the greenhouse. It was big, covered with a dark plastic material, and locked tight.

"Isn't the idea of a greenhouse to let the light in?" I said.

"Yeah, unless it's being lit from inside," Josie said.

"You think he's growing weed?" I said, scanning the outside of the greenhouse for any gaps that would let me take a peek inside.

"That would be my guess," Josie said. "And judging by the size of that thing, he's growing a lot of it." She looked around, then back at me. "Now what?"

"Well, I'm not sure. Now we know who lives here. And we know that Carl and Chef Claire have got something going on. And that his interest in gardening isn't confined to lawns and flowers."

"I think we should probably get out of here. I don't think we're going to learn anything else tonight. And I have no interest in watching them. Besides, I'm hungry."

"We could knock on the door. Maybe they'd invite us in for dinner," I said, laughing.

"Sure. Excuse us, Carl, but we were just passing by and thought we smelled chilidogs."

Josie chuckled under her breath; then I heard a low guttural sound.

"Say, Josie?"

"What?"

"How hungry are you?"

"I could eat."

"No, I mean, is that your stomach growling?"

90

"I thought that was you," she said. "Uh-oh."

"It's a dog isn't it?" I said, glancing over my shoulder.

"That would be my guess," she whispered. "A big dog."

The growl, coming from right behind us, intensified.

"Sounds like a Rottweiler," Josie said.

"Yup," Josie said. "Okay, Dog Whisperer, time for you to do your thing."

"I was hoping you'd have a suggestion. How do you want to play it?" I said, finally able to make out the beast's outline in the darkness.

"Very slowly," she said, reaching into the pocket of her jacket.

The dog started barking. Josie tossed a dog biscuit onto the ground. The dog stopped barking, and we heard a short burst of chewing. Then the beast barked twice before resuming the guttural growl. The front door opened, and Carl stepped onto the front stoop.

"Max," Carl shouted.

The dog stopped barking and cocked its head at the voice.

"What is it, Carl?"

I recognized Chef Claire's voice, and she appeared, half-dressed, next to Carl in the doorway.

"He's probably got something cornered out there. There's been a raccoon hanging around that's been driving him nuts."

"You need to go out there and get him?"

"Nah, he'll probably be fine as long as it isn't a skunk or a porcupine."

"You want to make sure, or would you like a little appetizer before dinner?" Chef Claire said, wrapping her arms around his waist.

"What do you think?" he said, turning around and leading her back inside.

"Ah, the power of lust," Josie said, then she turned and came face to face with the beast. "Max. Who's the good boy?"

91

Max wasn't in the mood to chit-chat. He sat on his haunches and continued to growl as he stared at Josie. She tossed another biscuit in his direction. He snatched it out of mid-air and swallowed it whole.

"Well, that's all I got," Josie said.

"Hand me those biscuits," I said, summoning up my courage.

"Be careful," Josie said, handing me the small plastic bag filled with dog biscuits. "You could lose a hand."

"Nah, he's a good boy," I said, slowly approaching the dog. "Aren't you, Max?"

The beast continued to growl, but it had softened. I slowly reached my closed hand forward, and Max stopped growling long enough to take a sniff. I then opened my hand and showed him the biscuit. He gently removed it from my hand, gulped it down, then sat at my feet and waited for another. I repeated the process. After three cookies, I rubbed his head and scratched his ears. I gave him another biscuit and Max decided he wanted a tummy rub. I scratched his stomach and gave him one more biscuit. I gave his head a final rub then stood and wiped my hands on my jeans.

"Unbelievable," Josie said. "How do you do that?"

"I speak dog," I said, laughing. "You ready to get out of here?"

"Absolutely."

I began removing the rest of the biscuits from the bag. I gave one to the dog, then tossed them one at a time towards the greenhouse at varying distances. Max trotted off to start hunting them down.

"Let's go," I said, starting the trek back toward the car. "What a cute dog."

"I'm starving. Let's pick up a pizza on the way home," Josie said.

"Oooh, that sounds good," I said, also feeling a hunger pang. "So what do we do with this new piece of information?"

"File it away for now and just keep poking around?" Josie said, shrugging.

"Yeah, that usually works," I said, laughing. "I guess there's just one more question we need to answer tonight."

"What's that?"

"You want to get an extra large with pepperoni and mushrooms?"

"You read my mind."

"Just call me the Vet Whisperer."

Chapter 16

Sammy, our new summer hire, continued to impress us with his work ethic and love for dogs. As such, Josie and I had decided to accelerate his training and increase his responsibilities. At the moment, I was explaining how we put together our daily schedule as we toured the back section of the Inn where the dog condos were located. It was taking a while since I insisted on starting each morning personally visiting each dog to say hello.

Some of my staff thought I was nuts to spend up to two hours rubbing bellies and getting licks and kisses from our diverse collection of four-legged fur balls, but if you can think of a better way to start the day, let me know. Chloe, trailing close behind, seemed to enjoy saying good morning as well.

"Outside each condo, you'll see that dog's chart," I said, handing one to Sammy. "The first thing you need to do is confirm whether the dog is a boarder, is here for a medical reason, or is one of our rescues."

"Got it," Sammy said, entering a note on his iPad.

"After you've done that, you need to cross reference it with Josie's schedule for the day. If any of the dogs have a medical procedure scheduled, we don't feed them in the morning, and we don't let them outside to run with the other dogs."

"When can they resume their regular schedule?"

"That's a very good question, Sammy."

"Thanks," he said, beaming.

"Josie makes comments on each chart, and you should always check that first if you have any questions. And at the end of each day, we have a meeting where we review the day and discuss tomorrow's schedule. It usually starts around five, and you should be there today."

"Is Josie at these meetings?" Sammy said, trying but failing to sound casual.

Here we go. Another one completely smitten with Josie. I could set my watch by it. Meet Josie; fall in love. Unfortunately for him, being seventeen, Sammy would forever be confined to the realm of fantasy when it came to her. But I didn't feel the need to discourage him. After all, he's seventeen. And if you can't dream big when you're seventeen, what chance does one have?

"Yes, she'll be there," I said. "She runs the meeting. So pay attention."

"Oh, I will," Sammy said, making another note. "I'll be there at four thirty."

"We'll be there at five," I said, smiling at him as I stopped to brush a burr out of a collie's tail whose owners were on vacation. "Good girl. You're such a good girl, Sophie."

"You're really good with all of them," Sammy said. "I mean, I've never seen anybody who handles dogs like you do."

"Thanks, Sammy. That's very nice of you to say," I said, glancing around the set of condos. "Okay, it's time for their morning meal. Don't forget to check the water system to make sure it's refilling all their bowls. We had a problem with it a couple of weeks ago."

I led him to the far wall of the room.

"Remember, the green button that says Out opens all the condos so the dogs can go outside. After they've eaten, let them out per the schedule for a couple of hours. There's no rain in the forecast today so they should be fine. When it's raining, we use the button that says Inside to open all the doors on this side of the condos, and we take all the dogs to the playroom down the hall."

"Must be nice," Sammy said. "They live better than I do."

95

"Oh, always check all the outside gates to make sure none of them have been left open. And keep an eye on how the German shepherd and Doberman are getting along today. They had a bit of a dust-up yesterday over a toy they both wanted."

Sammy's fingers flew over the touchpad as he tried to keep up.

"I think I got it," he said.

"Okay," I said, heading toward the door that led back in the reception area with Chloe at my heels. "Let me know if you have any questions."

Inside the waiting area, I saw Josie exit one of the exam rooms and gave her a quick update on my time with Sammy. When I mentioned *smitten*, she laughed and shook her head.

"Just be gentle with him," I said.

"He's a good kid. And cute." Josie said, then her attention shifted to the front door.

Marge Crawford stepped inside, removed her sunglasses, and frowned. Apparently, visiting an establishment for dogs was way down her list of favorite things to do. She spotted us and approached.

"Good morning," she said.

"Hi, Marge," I said.

"Please address me as Mrs. Crawford," she said, glancing around the room and sniffing as if she were trying to determine the source and direction of the smell. "Is there somewhere we can talk in private?"

"Sure," I said, gesturing for her to follow us into my office.

"What is that smell?" she said as she sat down and draped one leg over the other.

I looked at Josie, who shrugged back at me.

"Dog, I guess," I said, sitting down behind my desk. "How can we help you, Mrs. Crawford?"

"This is a bit delicate," she said.

96

"I see," I said.

Chloe hopped up onto my lap and stared across the desk at her. I scratched her ears and waited.

"I've been looking for something on the island and haven't had any luck. I'm at my wit's end. That's why I'm here."

"Why would you come here?" Josie said.

"The object I'm looking for is quite small, and I'm wondering... Well, since that dog-"

"Chloe," I said.

"Yes, whatever. Chloe," she said, waving me off. "Since the dog and my ex-husband were apparently inseparable before he drowned, and I've run out of places to look, I'm wondering if it's possible that she may have eaten it."

I glanced at Josie, who was leaning forward listening closely.

"What exactly is it that you think Chloe might have eaten?" I said.

"A key?"

"What kind of key?"

"It's just a key. Probably a small one."

"Why do you think Chloe could have eaten it?"

"I just told you. I've looked everywhere, and I'm running out of places to look," she snapped. "I'm sorry. I'm just so frustrated."

"I understand," I said, my patience with her rapidly disappearing.

"Aren't puppies always eating things they shouldn't?"

"Well, sure," I said. "But dogs usually start by chewing things that feel good on their teeth. You know, leather shoes, table legs-"

"The legs of women who don't like dogs," Josie interjected, forcing a smile at Mrs. Crawford.

Mrs. Crawford glared at Josie but chose to ignore the insult.

"Isn't it possible that she ate a key?"

97

"She's a dog, not a billy goat," I said.

"How can you be sure without checking her...well, you know. Didn't you check her stools?"

I glanced at Josie before responding. She was getting as annoyed as I was.

"We usually aren't that up close and personal with our guests," I said, smiling at her. "I mean, a girl's got to have her privacy, right?"

If Marge thought my joke was funny, she did a good job of not showing it.

"Surely you must have someone on staff responsible for that sort of thing."

"No, I'm afraid we don't," Josie said. "If you'd like to check for yourself, I can take you out to the poo-pile. But I should warn you to prepare yourself, it's quite an extensive collection."

"And you might want to change your shoes first," I said. "I don't recommend going open-toed."

She glared at both of us and started tapping her foot on the floor. For several seconds, it was the only sound as our staredown played out.

"Look, Mrs. Crawford, when we found Chloe, the first thing Josie did was take x-rays to make sure she was okay. And if anything like a key showed up, Josie would have removed it."

"Well, okay," she said, standing up. "I guess it was a long shot. But if anything turns up, be sure to let me know. I need to find that key."

"What's the key for?" I said, unable to resist.

"Do you think that's any of your business?" she said, lifting her sunglasses to stare at me.

"No, but if we only knew what kind of key it was, it might help us know what to look for," I said.

"Would it now?" she said, dismissing me with a wave of her hand. She pushed her sunglasses back in place and strode off out of the Inn.

"Nice try," Josie said, laughing. "If we only knew what kind of key it was?"

"So it wasn't my best effort," I said, shrugging. "But that was definitely a sign of desperation on her part, wouldn't you say?

"Yes, it was. I guess the rumors of a new will floating around might be accurate."

"But if she did it, and I'm beginning to think she did, why would she kill him off before she got her hands on it?" I said.

Josie got up and poured two cups of coffee. She handed one to me, then sat back down. I repositioned the sleeping Chloe and carefully took a sip.

"If Chef Claire is right that the divorce wasn't final, there's a good chance she'd end up being able to keep everything for herself," Josie said. "Unless there is a new will floating around."

"Again, but why would she kill him off before she got her hands on the new will? If Crawford were the only one who knew about it, she'd need him around to find out where it was, right?"

Josie nodded and sipped her coffee. We sat in silence thinking it through.

"Maybe she just lost control in a fit of anger. Maybe she caught Crawford in the act with Roxanne, and it brought back a bunch of bad memories. Unrequited love and all that sort of thing."

"Nah, I'm not buying it," I said. "You saw Marge at dinner the other night. She obviously can't stand Roxanne, but I didn't pick up on any jealousy."

"No, me neither," Josie said. "Total hatred, maybe. But not jealousy."

"And if she hates Roxanne that much, why not just kill her instead of Crawford?"

99

"She obviously considers Roxanne pond scum, but Marge doesn't seem like someone who would kill somebody just because she didn't like them."

"No, Marge seems to be the type who would figure out a way to keep someone like Roxanne around just to make her life miserable," I said. "You know, show Roxanne who was the boss."

Josie nodded and set her empty cup on my desk. Chloe heard the noise and woke long enough to glance up, then tucked her head under my arm and went back to sleep.

"I think we're missing something," I said.

"I don't have any doubts about it," Josie said.

I laughed and leaned back in my chair.

"Crawford's *accident* happened on the River, right?"

"Yeah. Either that or it happened somewhere else, and he was taken out in a boat and tossed overboard."

"But either way, Crawford was a big guy. And he would have been a load to get in and out of a boat. Marge doesn't look strong enough to have taken him out and gotten him into the water all by herself."

"Maybe she took him by surprise," Josie said.

"Perhaps. But Marge doesn't seem like the type to sneak up on someone. She's an in-your-face kind of girl."

"She certainly is. So that takes us back to what we were talking about the other day. She had help."

"Yup," I said.

"You know what you need to do, right?" Josie said.

I slowly nodded my head and stared out the window.

"Call Jerry the Lawyer."

"Exactly."

"The things I do around here," I said.

100

"If you like, we can just forget the whole thing and get on with our lives," Josie said, raising an eyebrow.

"You know I can't do that," I said.

"Okay then. You do get all the fun jobs, don't you?" Josie said, laughing.

"How do you think I should play it?"

"I'd go seductive," Josie said, grabbing a handful of candy from the jar on my desk. "You know, show some leg. Put the twins on display."

"He's going to get the wrong idea," I said.

"If you're going to be working him for information, you want him wanting and weak."

"Wanting and weak?"

"It's the clinical term for horny," she said, munching on a piece of chocolate.

I snorted, then picked up Chloe and put her on the floor. I stood and stretched.

"I guess I've done worse things," I said.

"And you'll be on your own. Think you can handle it?"

"Sure. A piece of cake."

"Cake? What a great idea. I need to run out at lunchtime. I'll swing by Pattersons and pick one up."

"I wish you'd gain a couple of pounds at some point."

101

Chapter 17

I walked inside Tondeuse and paused to let my eyes adjust to the light. Chef Michael was reviewing that evening's reservations with the hostess but looked up when he saw me and smiled.

"Hi, Suzy," he said. "Nice to see you. And your date is already here."

"Hi, Chef," I said, glancing around the main dining room for signs of Jerry the Lawyer.

"I've got you at a nice romantic table in the back room," he said.

"Romantic? That wasn't necessary, Chef."

"Really? Your mom called earlier and said this was a special night."

"She did, huh?" I said, fuming. "She has a tendency to overstate things."

"Well, regardless, I'm sure you'll enjoy what we've got set up for you. And there won't be a piece of fish within a hundred feet," he said, laughing.

"That's a good start, Chef. Thanks."

I made my way to the table and, as promised, Jerry was already there, staring out the window. He stood when he saw me, checked my legs out, and held my chair as I sat down. I placed the napkin across my lap and looked across the table at him. He was already pouring champagne into my glass. He placed the bottle back in the ice bucket and smiled.

"Your mom bought it for us," he said.

"Of course," I said, taking a sip. It was very good. Mom was pulling out all the stops tonight.

"I have to admit that I was surprised when you called. Your mom said you might, but I thought she was just trying to be nice."

"My mother being nice? Doubtful."

"I like her," Jerry said. "She's a real straight shooter. They're pretty rare these days." He took another sip of champagne. Since I didn't respond, he felt the need to agree with himself and nodded. "Yeah, they broke the mold when they made her."

"I think she was the one who shattered it."

Jerry laughed and leaned forward. He placed both his hands over mine. I bit my lip and freed one of my hands to grab my glass. I was at a loss as to how to get the other one loose.

"So, let's talk about us," he said, gazing into my eyes.

"Sure," I said. "That shouldn't take too long."

Jerry let go of my hand and sat back in his chair. He gave me an odd smile.

"You look great tonight," he said.

"Thanks," I said.

"So why did you agree to a second date?"

"Actually, this one is more like date one-and-a-half. Our first one ran out of steam pretty early."

"Yeah, it did," he said. "I blame my buddy Frederick. He has a tendency to get things off track if you know what I mean."

"Good idea," I said, forcing a smile. "Let's blame Frederick. So, how much longer are you going to be in town?"

He thought about the question for a long time before answering. Why I have no idea. It seemed like an easy one.

"Probably until early next week. That is, assuming I can get everything here wrapped up."

"You mean whatever you're doing for Marge Crawford?"

"Yeah," he said, glancing away, then refocusing on my cleavage.

"What exactly are you doing for old Marge?"

103

"Oh, basic stuff," he said, casually fiddling with his glass. "Just trying to make sure she gets everything she deserves."

"Like all of her dead ex-husband's money?"

"Wow," Jerry said. "You don't pull any punches, do you?"

I decided to slow down and back off a bit. There was no sense in putting him completely on the defensive this early in the evening. Since I was starving, that could wait until dessert.

"It was just that it was obvious the other night at dinner that things are pretty strained around that island at the moment. And nobody seemed to be grieving. So I assumed that everyone was there for another reason. Since he was worth hundreds of millions, I came to the conclusion that the money was their reason for being there."

"Who ever really knows the motives of others? And people grieve in different ways," he said with a small shrug.

"Yes, they do," I said, taking a small sip of champagne. "But it doesn't usually manifest itself in open hostility and hatred."

Jerry laughed. Despite the fact that I found him to be a cloying narcissist, I had to concede that he had a great laugh. I smiled and felt a tinge of warmth for him. I cursed myself and vowed to go slow with the bubbly.

"I have to agree with you. The wicked ex-wife, the ex-hooker girlfriend, and the jack of all trades gardener who looks like he just stepped off the cover of a bad romance novel. It's quite a collection."

"Not to mention the straight-laced corporate zombie," I said, nodding.

Jerry's eyes narrowed, and he frowned.

"I've never spent much time with her. But she's a real piece of work, too," he said.

"Rosaline, right?"

"That's her."

104

He had an interesting reaction to my mention of Rosaline. I studied Jerry's face, and it held the same expression he'd had during our first date when he realized he wasn't going to get anywhere with me. If he'd put the moves on Rosaline and struck out, when had that happened? It could have been at dinner when I'd been in the kitchen stuffing my face with chili dogs. I made a mental note to ask Josie if she'd seen anything that night and filed it away.

Our waitress arrived with a plate of stuffed mushrooms and salads.

"I don't think we ordered these, Michelle," I said, glancing up at her.

"Your mom called in your order this afternoon," she said, smiling.

"Of course she did," I said, glancing at Jerry.

"In case you're wondering, you're both having the New York, medium-rare, with a side of penne in red sauce. And your chocolate soufflés will be going in the oven as soon as I bring your entrees."

"Thanks, Michelle."

She waved casually and walked off. I took a sip of champagne and sat quietly fuming.

"Dinner sounds great," Jerry said.

"Yeah, it's my favorite meal."

"Then why the long face, Seabiscuit?"

I laughed at his joke and felt myself relaxing.

"It's just my mother," I said. "Do you ever feel like your mother is constantly hovering over you like a drone?"

"Actually, no," he whispered.

I'd somehow managed to touch another soft spot, but I felt bad about this one. I decided to get back to why I was there in the first place.

"You referred to Mrs. Crawford as the *wicked* ex-wife. That's an interesting choice of words."

"You were there at dinner. What word would you use to describe her?"

105

"Wicked works. But Mrs. Crawford is one of your clients."

"Listen, if one of my clients isn't wicked, that's when I get nervous. And if I limited my practice to only those who walk a straight line, I'd be in the poor house. Of course, I'm not necessarily suggesting your mother is wicked by any means."

"That's okay," I said. "If the ruby slipper fits, right?"

He laughed softly and stared off into the distance. "Marge Crawford is one of the worst I've ever come in contact with, but..."

"But what?"

"She pays well, and she pays on time."

"I guess that's important in your line of work," I said, nibbling a mushroom.

"In my line of work, that's everything."

"It sounds kind of sad," I said, starting work on my salad.

"Maybe I should get a dog," he said, popping a mushroom into his mouth.

"A little unconditional love probably couldn't hurt," I said, studying him closely.

"Unconditional love? What planet are you from?" he snapped. Then he exhaled loudly and wiped his mouth with his napkin. "I'm sorry. That was uncalled for. I think I could use a healthy dose of whatever bottle of compassion you're drinking from."

"Forget it," I said. "It doesn't matter."

"I just have a lot on my mind lately."

"There's a lot of that going around these days. Tell me something, Jerry. If you weren't a lawyer, what would you like to do?"

"Easy one. I'd buy a boat, head for the Caribbean, and start a charter fishing business."

"What's stopping you?"

"Unfinished business, I guess."

"Maybe you'll get it finished soon, huh?"

"That would be great," he said, glancing up at our waitress arriving with our steaks. "Here we go."

We waited as she set our plates down and poured two glasses of red wine from an already opened bottle of Caymus Cabernet. I shook my head, then glanced up and smiled at the waitress.

"She ordered the wine as well," she said, laughing.

"Of course she did," I said, taking a sip. It was delicious.

"The woman certainly knows her wine," Jerry said, cutting into his steak.

"If I can ask, what exactly are you doing for my mother?"

"I can't go into any details, but she's just making sure all her affairs are in order."

"That's a lot of affairs to keep track of," I said, laughing.

"What?"

"Nothing. Inside joke. So are they in order?"

"They are now," he said, nodding. "Don't worry, you're going to like it."

"It doesn't matter to me one way or another," I said. "I'll probably end up spending whatever she leaves me on dogs."

"That would be a lot of dogs," he said, taking another bite of steak. "This is really good."

"It is," I said. "Like I said, it doesn't matter."

"It would matter to me," he said. "Do you have any idea how rich your mother is?"

"No, I don't."

That was the truth, I didn't. But I did know that there were several zeros on the tail end of her bank account.

"Well, she's loaded. It's certainly not Crawford money, but she can hold her own in some serious company."

"So, you're only after me for my money?"

I don't know why I said it, but somehow it worked to lighten the mood that had descended over our table.

"Wow," he said, setting his knife and fork down on his plate. "Am I dreaming, or did you just turn playful."

"It must be the wine," I said, embarrassed.

"Don't stop. I like it," he said, beaming at me. "But to answer your question, no, I'm not after your money. Which, by the way, you probably won't have for years."

"Then it must be my charming personality," I said, giggling.

"I'll let you know as soon as I see it," he said.

I knew he was joking, but the comment still made me a bit cranky. I sipped my wine and glanced around the restaurant.

"Don't get mad," he said. "You have to admit you're pretty tough on people."

"Do you really think so?"

"Well, you certainly have been tough on me."

"Yes, I have," I said. "But I attribute that to the fact that going out with you was my mother's idea. And you're a lawyer."

"You don't like lawyers?"

"No, as a general rule, I don't."

"But if we'd somehow just met, and I was a charter fishing boat captain, I'd have a shot?"

"Oh, you'd have more than a shot," I said.

Wow, where did that come from?

108

"Interesting," he said, starting to reach for my hand, then he stopped. He opted for a lustful gaze across the table. "This is where I usually try to be clever and say something like *your place or mine.*"

"Please tell me you're not going to do that," I said as my defensives went back on full alert.

"No, at least not tonight."

He continued to stare at me. I felt confused and flustered. That was all I needed. Here I was sitting at a table with someone who could have been involved in a murder, and I was about to start making goo-goo eyes at him.

I cursed the wine.

I cursed my mother.

I cursed him for being so darn cute.

I needed to get out of here right now.

Well, right after the soufflé.

On cue, our waitress arrived carrying two chocolate delights that smelled incredible. She set them down in front of us.

"Can I bring you an after dinner cocktail to go with the soufflé?"

"No, thanks, Michelle. Just coffee, please. And keep it coming."

Chapter 18

Chloe sneezed then shook vigorously throwing shampoo in several directions including all over Josie and me. We both laughed as Chloe sneezed twice more then sat and waited for me to continue.

"She loves getting a bath," Josie said.

"Yeah, and that's good news for us. I'd hate to see the mess if she didn't," I said, wiping my face and arms with a towel.

Josie checked her schedule on her phone then slid it back into her scrubs. "I've got fifteen minutes before my next appointment. So tell me all about your date."

"It wasn't a date, it was just dinner," I said, working on a chunk of mud crammed tight between one of Chloe's front paws. "How the heck did you get so muddy?"

If Chloe remembered, she wasn't telling.

"So?" Josie said, raising an eyebrow at me.

"So what?"

"Details. I need some details," Josie said, grabbing the hose and starting the rinse process.

"Well, my mother took the liberty of ordering for us."

"Of course," Josie said, nodding as she rinsed Chloe's back legs.

"And since she couldn't help sticking her nose into my business, I stuck her with the check."

"Good for you," Josie said. "But that's not the kind of detail I was looking for."

"I know what you're looking for," I said.

"Well?"

"I actually had a better time that I thought I would," I said, glancing over my shoulder at her.

"Really? He didn't do his shtick?"

"His *shtick*?"

"You know, work his game on you."

"A little at first, yeah," I said, flashing back on the hand grabbing across the table. "But then he settled down and became a real person for a while."

"That's good," she said, turning the hose off and tossing me a fresh towel. "He's cute as all get out."

"Yes, he certainly is," I said, drying Chloe's head.

"Are you going to see him again?"

"I'm not sure that's a good idea. I don't think he's involved in the Crawford mess, but-"

"Why don't you think he's involved?"

"He hates Marge Crawford. He's doing work for her, what exactly I'm still not sure, but he says it's because she pays him a lot of money to do it."

"You believe him?" Josie said, drying off Chloe's back legs.

"Yeah, I think I do," I said. "What possible motive could he have to do something like that?"

"You just said it. She's paying him a lot of money."

"I imagine he has more than enough money. And if Marge were dead, she wouldn't be able to pay him anymore, right?"

"You've got a point there," Josie said.

"I don't know what it is, but he doesn't seem to be that type of person."

"Then you should probably go out with him again, right?"

"Yeah, maybe," I said. "I don't know. But he's not a dog person. That's never a good sign. I need to think about it."

Josie laughed and tossed the used towel into a nearby bin.

111

"What's so funny?"

"You. I know that look. It's the one you use when you're about to go back into hiding."

"I'm not hiding," I said. "I'm just cautious."

Josie laughed again. Despite my fondness for all things Josie, she was starting to make me cranky.

"You're one to talk," I said.

"Leave me out of this," she said, washing her hands. She fiddled with her hair in the mirror above the sink as she dried her hands. "But don't worry. The next time I meet someone who gets my motor running, you'll know all about it. And I certainly won't be playing Hide and Seek," she said, staring at me through the mirror.

"I said I'd think about it," I said, getting ready to put Chloe's collar back on her. After three tries, I gave up. "Well, I love this collar, but I think it's time for a new one. She's outgrown it."

"Let me see it," Josie said.

I tossed her the collar and resumed working on Chloe with the towel. She loved it and wanted to play.

"Hang in there, girl," I said, patting her head dry with the towel. "That's a good girl."

"This one's toast," Josie said, examining the ornate collar. "There's just no room to punch another hole in it." She glanced at Chloe. "You're just growing up too fast, aren't you?"

Chloe wagged her tail, then sat down expecting her collar to be put back in place. She looked back and forth at us, then barked once.

"Hold your horses," I said, laughing.

I glanced at Josie expecting her also to be enjoying the moment, but she was focused on the collar. She ran a hand along the inside of the collar, then squeezed it in several places.

112

"What is it?" I said.

"I think there's something inside the collar," she said, handing it to me.

"The lining probably just came loose," I said, turning it over in my hand.

"No, I don't think so. It's a solid object."

"That's strange," I said as I held it up to the light. Why I have no idea. It was made of heavy cloth and leather and was about half an inch thick. I caught the smile Josie was giving me and felt my face flush with embarrassment.

"Good one, Sherlock," Josie said. "We could just cut it open and find out."

"No, I don't want to destroy it if we don't have to. I want it as a keepsake," I said, continuing to examine the collar. "Now that I think about it, she has been scratching at it the past couple of days."

Josie glanced up at the clock, then opened the door.

"Sammy. Got a minute?"

Sammy entered and waved hello to me. He patted Chloe on the head and rubbed the back of her ears. "What's up?"

"Look, I'm going to need a few minutes," Josie said. "Is Mrs. Everly here yet?"

"Big woman with blue hair?"

"Yes, that's her," Josie said. "She's brought Brutus in for his annual checkup. Could you get them into exam room four, pull his chart, and weigh him? I'll be right in."

"I don't know. He's a pretty big dog," Sammy said, nervously. "Does he bite?"

"Only when people try to weigh him," Josie said, straight-faced. "I'm joking, Sammy. Don't worry, Brutus will love you."

"Okay, room four, got it," he said, backing out of the room.

113

"Are you ready?" Josie said, taking the collar out of my hand.

"For what?"

"To take an x-ray of the collar, of course."

"What a good idea," I said following Josie out the door. Chloe trailed at my heels. "I don't know why I didn't think of that."

"Your mind is obviously on something else. Or should I say, *someone* else?"

"Drop it," I said, punching her on the arm.

Josie headed straight for the x-ray area while I picked Chloe up and stepped inside a small office a safe distance away from the machine. Five minutes later she returned carrying the collar and the x-ray. She snapped it into place on a display unit on the wall and turned on the light.

Stunned, we both stared at the image.

"So Mrs. Crawford was right," Josie said.

"Yeah, Chloe had it all the time," I said, picking up the collar. "I guess we'll have to cut it open."

"I'm afraid so," Josie said, rummaging through one of the drawers. She removed a scalpel, and I handed her the collar. "Don't worry. I'll try not to ruin it."

I watched as she expertly cut along the edge of the collar then peeled it open. She removed the object and held it up. The gold key glistened in the light.

"What kind of key is it?" I said.

"Safe deposit box would be my guess."

I nodded.

"Now what?" Josie said, handing me the key.

"I guess we should return it," I said.

"You're dying to get another look at that island, aren't you?"

"No, I'm just trying to be a good citizen. You know, returning things to their rightful owner," I said.

It sounded so insincere even I laughed when I heard myself say it.

"So, I guess this officially puts Mrs. Crawford right at the top of our suspect's list," Josie said.

"It certainly does. Marge knew the key existed. And I'm betting that whatever is locked away could do some real damage to her plans."

"A new will?" Josie said, sitting down.

"Or the original one?"

"Could be. Or maybe a copy of the mysterious divorce settlement Chef Claire mentioned?"

"That's a good thought," I said. "If it was signed and the divorce is final, and if Mrs. Crawford could get her hands on the original and destroy it, wouldn't everything go to her?"

"People could try to fight it, but Marge would be in a pretty strong position," Josie said.

"How's your afternoon look?"

Josie pulled out her phone and checked her schedule. "It opens up after lunch."

"Feel like taking a boat ride this afternoon?"

"You read my mind," Josie said.

"How about you Chloe? You want to go for a ride later on?"

Chloe barked once and wagged her tail.

"I think she likes the idea," Josie said, laughing.

"The scary part is that I think she understood what I was saying," I said.

"When you get a chance, ask Chloe what she thinks you should do about Jerry the Lawyer," Josie said, laughing as she stood up. "I need to run.

I have a date with Brutus I'm late for." She paused at the door and turned back. "Should we pack a lunch for the ride?"

"I'll see what I can do," I said.

"Don't go to any trouble. But maybe the turkey club from Delmonte, with a side of potato salad, coleslaw, and a pickle. Oh, and a bag of brownies from Patersons. I love their brownies."

"Anything else?" I said, rolling my eyes.

"A diet Coke," she said. "I'm watching my calories."

She laughed all the way down the hall.

Chapter 19

I cut the engine, and we began drifting in the shallows about a mile from downtown Clay Bay. The summer was in full swing, but the River was surprisingly quiet given the bright sun and calm water. Josie removed the large men's dress shirt she was wearing and stepped out of her shorts to reveal the two-piece bathing suit she was wearing. It was new, and its orange and pale blue pattern worked perfectly with her skin tone. It was by no means a micro-bikini, and it covered her as well as the two pieces of fabric could, but it was fighting a losing battle. You'd need a car cover to hide that body. I shook my head.

"What?" she said, catching my reaction.

"You. Nobody should look that good. Especially given the amount of food you eat."

"Thanks. It's just good genes. You've seen my grandmother. And don't be too hard on yourself. You look great." She pulled her Blue Jays hat further down and adjusted her sunglasses. "But speaking of food."

I tossed her the bag of sandwiches, and she began unpacking our lunch. Chloe went on point. I grabbed an apple and removed the core and seeds and cut it into small slices. I laid them out on a plate and set it down in front of her. She wagged her tail and began working her way through her snack.

"She eats like a lady," Josie said, observing the meticulous manner Chloe selected and chewed each slice.

"She gets that from her mother," I said.

"What's that supposed to mean?" Josie said through a mouthful of her club sandwich.

117

I took a bite of my sandwich and looked around. The setting was more than beautiful. It was perfect. A gentle breeze kicked up, and the sun was hot. I leaned back against the cushion and knew if I stayed in that position very long, I'd be napping.

I heard the boat before I saw it. Chloe heard it too and began a low growl I'd never heard from her before.

"What's the matter, girl?" I said, setting my sandwich down next to me.

She continued the low guttural growl, and I leaned down to pick her up. Chloe continued to stare at the boat as it drew closer. It was the first time I'd gotten a look at the boat since it was covered the two previous times we'd seen it in the boathouse. It was black and sleek with a modified V hull that provided both stability and flexibility for dealing with a variety of water conditions. The back half of the boat was open and would work well for transporting a variety of supplies and materials to the island. And from the low throaty growl of the engine, I knew it had a lot of power. At the moment, Chloe was doing her best to drown out the engine with her throaty growl.

"That's odd," Josie said as she tossed her sandwich wrapper back in the bag and started working on her potato salad.

"Yeah, she's never done that before," I said, continuing to watch the boat.

As it drew closer, I recognized Carl. We exchanged waves and Chloe also recognized him and stopped growling. But she continued to watch the boat closely. I got up and grabbed the side of Carl's boat as it came alongside ours.

"Hi, Suzy," he said. "I thought that was you. Hey, Chloe. Who's the good girl? Man, she's getting big." Carl looked away from the dog and got his first good look at Josie. "Wow."

"Did you say something, Carl?" I said, laughing.

118

"Sorry," he said, embarrassed by the involuntary outburst. "Hi, Josie."

"Hello, Carl," Josie said with a quick wave before returning to her potato salad.

"What are you up to?" I said.

"I'm just running a few errands."

"How are things at the island?" I said, picking up my sandwich before Chloe got any ideas.

"The usual," he said, laughing. "Intense hatred spiced with a bit of intrigue."

"Intrigue?"

"There's a feeling around the place like something big is about to happen, but nobody knows what it is or when it's going to happen," Carl said, sneaking a quick glance at Josie sitting on the thick cushion that ran the length of the stern. She was already making quick work of one of the brownies. "It's been quiet this morning, but I still used the excuse of running errands to get out of there."

"So, Mrs. Crawford is still there?" I said.

"Oh, yeah. I doubt if she's going anywhere for a while. At least not until she finishes what she calls her *recovery therapy*."

"You lost me, Carl," I said, taking a bite of my half-eaten turkey club. I needed to catch up and finish it before Josie worked her way through the whole bag of brownies.

"That's what she calls it," he said, continuing to grasp the side of our boat with one hand. "To me, it's what I've always called spring cleaning."

"Mrs. Crawford? Cleaning?" I said.

"Yup. She's cleaning everything. Right down to the inside of every cabinet and drawer in the house."

119

I nodded and glanced at Josie. For some reason, I didn't feel the need to tell Carl that not only did we know what she was looking for, but that it was safely tucked away in a plastic bag in my pocket.

"She doesn't seem like the type to spend a lot of her time cleaning," Josie said.

"That's what I thought," Carl said. "I offered to find her a cleaning crew to hire, but she said it was something she needed to do herself. That was when she used the term recovery therapy. I guess I get where she's coming from." He stood straight up and let go of our boat. "Besides, it looks like it might be her island now. She can do whatever she wants around the place. I need to run. It was nice seeing both of you." He glanced at me, then lingered on Josie.

"Why do you say it looks like it's hers?" I said, unable to resist that juicy tidbit. Josie even put her brownie down to listen.

"She says Crawford gave it to her in the divorce," Carl said, shrugging. "And I guess nobody has come up with any documentation to say he didn't. Mrs. Crawford says it's her word against his. I laughed when she said it because I thought it was funny. Nobody else did. I'll see you guys around."

He waved at us and slowly drove off in the direction of the public town dock.

"Do you think he's somehow playing us, or is Carl just a bit slow on the uptick?" Josie said.

"Yeah, that was odd, wasn't it?" I said, polishing off my sandwich and grabbing the last brownie from the bag. Chloe sat and stared at the brownie. "Sorry, girl. But no chocolate for you."

I looked at Josie, who was stretching out on the back cushion and holding her stomach.

"It doesn't seem fair that dogs aren't able to eat something as delicious as chocolate."

120

"More for us," Josie said, laughing. "Ugh, I ate too much. I'm full."

"Why would Carl feel the need to do that?"

"Well, if he was doing it intentionally, and I'm not sure he was, it's what criminals do," Josie said.

"I'm going to need a bit more, Josie."

Josie struggled to sit upright. She took a long sip of Diet Coke, then burped loudly. "Excuse me. Oh, that's much better. Criminals try to deflect attention, introduce some misdirection. You know, do anything to keep the light from shining on them."

"Based on the way he explained the situation, wouldn't that would mean he's working with Mrs. Crawford?"

"I guess it could," Josie said.

"But what does he have to gain?" I said, then shook my head. "Never mind. Dumb question. Money. Maybe lots of it."

"Or the island?" Josie said. "If she does own it, I can't see her ever wanting to spend any time there. It would be quite the parting gift for Carl if she's able to pull it off."

"Assuming she's trying to pull something off," I said, sneaking a piece of turkey I'd saved to Chloe.

"I saw that," Josie said. "Don't get her too used to people food."

"Turkey's good for her," I said, rubbing Chloe's head.

"Just not too much or you'll turn her into a total mooch."

"Okay, Doc. Whatever you say."

"What was with that growling?" Josie said. "I've never heard anything like that come from her."

"That was strange," I said. "But she stopped when she recognized Carl. So we know she wasn't growling at him."

"That means she was growling at the boat," Josie said.

"You know what that means, right?"

"That Chloe remembered being on that boat and had a bad experience that stuck with her."

"Yes," I said, "An experience like watching your owner get attacked and thrown overboard."

"Uh-huh."

"And also remembering being thrown overboard herself," I said.

"And left to struggle to survive in the water all night until we found her the next morning."

My stomach churned as I wondered how anyone could toss a defenseless puppy into the River in the dead of night. I tried to generate the same amount of outrage for the deceased Mr. Crawford but came up short. It was funny how that worked. I could watch twenty people get massacred in a movie but not come close to the degree of anger I felt if someone so much laid a finger on a defenseless animal. I've been known to come out of my seat in protest when that happened.

Josie stood and pulled on her shorts and buttoned her shirt. She sat back down and patted the seat. Chloe trotted over to her and jumped up on the seat. I took my cue and started the boat and headed for Candyland Island.

Chapter 20

I slowed as we approached the boathouse on the far side of the island. The boat slip at the far end was empty, which made sense since we'd just seen Carl in Clay Bay fifteen minutes ago. All the other slips were still full and seemed identical to the last time we'd been here. I pulled up to the dock, and Josie hopped out and tied the boat off. Chloe climbed onto the dock and led the way.

"The boat Carl's driving would have been perfect to use for taking care of Crawford," I said, walking next to Josie along the dock.

"It certainly would. And that would put to rest the myth of the sunken boat."

"Yeah. It's not surprising nobody found anything after the *accident*, huh? No stray boat cushions washed up on shore. No chunks of a shattered boat found floating."

"You think it's time we had a little chat with Mrs. Crawford?" Josie said, starting to climb the long flight of stone steps that led to the main house.

"Since we're about to give her the key she's been looking everywhere for," I said, gasping and making a silent vow to get back to the gym, "I think the least she can do is talk with us and answer a few questions."

"We need to go easy, though," Josie said. "Let's not go straight for the jugular with 'Would you mind telling us why you killed your husband, Marge?' Okay?"

"Yeah, don't worry," I said, reaching the top step and pausing to take several deep breaths. "I won't open with that one."

Josie laughed and hopped up the front steps onto the front porch. She and Chloe waited until I managed to drag myself up the final steps. Josie started to push the doorbell but stopped when she noticed the front door was partially open.

"What do you think?" she said.

"Let's ring the doorbell," I said, desperate for a few extra seconds to catch my breath.

Josie rang the bell, and it reverberated through the house. We waited several seconds and then Josie knocked loudly on the door. We waited some more, and Josie glanced at me. I shrugged, and we pushed the door open and stepped inside. The house seemed empty, but it sure was clean. In fact, it was spotless. If Mrs. Crawford ever decided to set up shop as a housekeeper, I had a place in mind she could start.

We walked through the foyer, calling out, but received no response. We entered the library and looked around.

"I don't think anybody's here," Josie said. "What do you want to do?"

"It's a big house," I said. "Maybe they just can't hear us. Let's keep looking for a bit."

"You're in the mood to do a little snooping, aren't you?"

"Maybe a little," I said. "But I prefer the term curious."

"I'm sure you do," she said, crossing the massive library and going through the door that led to the dining room. "No dirty dishes," Josie said, glancing around the table. "And the tablecloth is fresh."

"Man, this place is immaculate," I said. "She hasn't missed a spot. Let's take a look in the kitchen. Maybe Chef Claire is around somewhere."

I pushed the swinging door open and poked my head inside. I scanned the huge industrial kitchen that was empty and was about to let the door close when Chloe sat down in the doorway, refused to move and started barking.

124

"What is it, girl?" I said, kneeling down to scratch her ears. She shook my hand away and continued barking and started scratching at the tile floor.

"That's odd," Josie said.

I pushed the door open until I felt the latch catch. Chloe tentatively stepped through the doorway and barked as she took one step forward, then two steps back. She sat down and looked up at me and barked again.

"Okay, okay," I said. "I'll check it out."

I stepped into the kitchen and looked around.

"I don't see anything," I said.

Chloe continued to bark, and it was starting to get on my nerves. I shushed her and walked further into the kitchen until I reached the large granite island where I'd eaten dinner with Chef Claire. Further convinced the kitchen was empty, I was about to exit when I caught a glimpse of something on the floor on the other side of the island. I leaned over the island, and my turkey club threatened to return when I saw the body sprawled on the floor.

"Geez," I said, shaking my head. "Wow. What a mess."

"What is it?" Josie said, peering around the corner of the kitchen island. "Oh, no. That poor woman."

I stood next to Josie, picked up Chloe in my arms to keep her from tracking through the gooey mess on the floor and looked down at the vacant stare on Marge Crawford's face.

"She's dead, right?" I said.

"Oh, yeah," Josie said. "No doubt about it."

"And that's maple syrup mixed in with all the blood, isn't it?"

"That would be my guess," Josie said, reaching for her phone. "Isn't Jackson supposed to get back from his conference today?"

"I think that's right," I said, unable to take my eyes off the expression on Mrs. Crawford's face. "She looks surprised."

125

Josie glanced down, then nodded in agreement. "Yeah, she does. But I imagine catching a knife that big in the neck might come as a bit of a shock."

I shifted my eyes to the large chef's knife that was still embedded. Josie made the call, put the phone on speaker and set it down on the island.

"Hello," said the familiar voice.

"Hi, Jackson," Josie said.

"Did you call just to welcome me home? That was sweet of you. Hey, I was about to swing by the Inn and pick up Sluggo. Are you in the office?"

"No, actually I'm not. And you might want to hold off on picking Sluggo up for a while."

"I don't think I like the sound of this," Jackson said.

"No, you're not going to like it at all, Jackson," I said.

"Hey, Suzy. What are you guys up to?"

"We're at Candyland Island," I said.

"Should I ask why?"

"That question can probably wait. But you need to get over here. In an official capacity."

"You want to tell me why?" Jackson said.

"Not on the phone," I said. "But you'll understand as soon as you get here."

"Are you guys in any danger?"

"No, I don't think so," I said, glancing at Josie for confirmation.

"Okay, I'm on my way."

"Oh, and Jackson?" Josie said.

"Yes?"

"If you can track down Freddie, bring him along."

"And the state police, too," I chimed in.

Chapter 21

We were sitting on the front porch when we saw Jackson's police boat approach the island. I recognized Freddie Sands, the county medical examiner, and Alice, Jackson's summer intern we'd met the day we discovered the first body. Sitting in the back of the boat was a state policeman I didn't know.

"Alice the Intern is certainly getting quite the experience this summer," Josie said.

"She'll have lots of stories to tell back at school," I said.

"Yeah, right after she changes majors," Josie said.

I laughed but stopped when I remembered the tragic circumstances that had brought the police boat to the island. Respect for the dead and all that. I chided myself as I watched them walk up the long set of steps. I did allow myself a bit of self-satisfaction that I wasn't the only one who'd huffed and puffed their way up to the house.

"Hi, Jackson," I said, getting up out of my chair.

"Hi, Suzy. Josie, nice to see you as always," he said, nodding to both of us. "You both know Alice and Freddie. This is Joe Abrams from the state police.

The state policeman shook hands with both of us. Right on cue, he lingered on Josie. And Freddie hadn't taken his eyes off her since he stepped onto the porch.

"So what's going on?" Jackson said.

"Marge Crawford is dead," I said.

"The ex-wife?" Jackson said. "What's she doing here?"

"She's been in town for a while. Probably tying up some loose ends."

127

"I guess that makes sense," Jackson said. "Where's the body?"

"In the kitchen behind the island," I said, sitting back down.

"You didn't touch anything did you?" Jackson said.

"No. But you want to be careful when you go in," Josie said. "There's maple syrup all over the floor."

"Again with the maple syrup?" Freddie said.

"Weird," Jackson said. "Who else is around?"

"Nobody," Josie said. "At least we haven't seen anybody."

"Okay, here's what we'll do. You guys stay out here on the porch while we take a look. Then Joe and I will need to interview you separately while Freddie does his thing. Alice, you stick with me."

Everyone nodded, and we stayed sat on the porch and played with Chloe while we waited. Fifteen minutes later, Jackson and the state policeman escorted Josie and me to different rooms and spoke with us for about an hour. When they were satisfied we'd answered all their questions, and they had a lot, we sat back down on the porch and waited until the ME had finished his initial examination.

Freddie walked onto the porch just as two paramedics arrived lugging a stretcher up the steps. He gave them their instructions, and they entered the house. Five minutes later, we heard the throaty purr of a boat approaching the island. Moments later, Carl climbed the steps carrying several plastic bags. When he reached the porch, he looked around and seemed genuinely surprised to see all of us.

"What's up?" Carl said, setting the bags down on the porch.

"You're Carl, right?" Jackson said.

"Yes, and you're Jackson. We had a couple of beers together one night around Christmas last year."

"That's right. At the Water's Edge. If I remember, you're a gardener."

"Among other things," he said. "So, what's going on?"

128

"Marge Crawford. I'm sorry to have to tell you that she's dead."

"What?" Carl stumbled backward until he came to rest against the railing. He seemed to be in total shock and if he was putting on an act, it was a good one.

"I'll need to speak with you, sir," the state policeman said.

"Sure. Of course," Carl said, following him into the house.

A few minutes later, the paramedics pushed the stretcher onto the porch. Thankfully, the body bag was zipped shut. I watched them carefully work their way down the steps, then looked at the ashen Alice who was staring off into the distance.

"Are you okay?" I said.

Alice turned and eventually managed to focus on me. "Yeah, I think so. It's just that this one is a lot harder to deal with than the guy in the water."

"It's all the blood," Josie said.

"There was so much of it," Alice said, sitting down in the glider. Chloe hopped up on her lap and started licking her hand. "And I'll never get the sight of that knife out of my head. Who could do something like that?"

"I'm not sure," Freddie said, holding up a plastic bag with the murder weapon inside. "But we will soon. I pulled a great set of prints."

"Really?" Josie said. "The killer left a set of prints? That was pretty careless wouldn't you say?"

"I don't think we're dealing with a genius here, Josie," Freddie said. "And at first glance, I think our suspect is a woman. The prints are pretty small."

"Let's hope that makes our job a bit easier," Jackson said. "Okay, I'll need to get a list of people who've been on the island from Carl." Then he glanced back and forth at Josie and me. "And I'm sorry to do this, ladies, but I'll need to get a set of prints from both of you."

"You're joking, right?" I said with a snort.

129

"There's no need to get snarky, Suzy. I just need to make sure I follow the normal procedure."

"All right," I said, nodding. "That ink does wash off doesn't it?"

"Yeah, in a couple of days, you'll be good as new," he said, laughing at his joke.

"How about a little respect for the dead, Jackson?"

He didn't get the reference and gave me a blank stare. Then I remembered that had been a conversation I'd had with myself. As you've probably figured out by now, I have a tendency to do that.

Chapter 22

After we finally left the island, I wandered around the Inn the rest of the afternoon into the early evening in a daze. I did my best to deal with whatever issues the staff presented as well as meet and greet our customers the way I always did, but my smiles felt forced. I finally gave up and headed to the back of the Inn to tour the condos and say hello to all our four-legged guests. After that, I felt somewhat refreshed and retreated into my office and stretched out on the couch with Chloe draped over my chest sleeping.

Josie wandered in soon after I'd settled in and she sat down and put her feet up on the desk. I opened one eye and nodded at her.

"That was one wild afternoon," Josie said. "Next time, let's just go fishing."

"You don't have to convince me," I said, adjusting the pillow under my head. My movements must have interrupted Chloe's beauty sleep because she snorted and kicked her legs as she repositioned herself.

"You do realize that if we'd shown up a half hour earlier, we could have both ended up on the floor next to Marge," Josie said.

"I'm trying not to think about it," I said.

"So I guess we're back to square one on the question of who killed Crawford," Josie said.

"Yeah, we can officially take Marge off our list of suspects."

I conceded the battle for couch dominance and gently moved Chloe off my chest and sat up. Chloe took full advantage of my weakness and stretched out even further. She sighed and began to snore softly.

"Who do you think did it?" Josie said.

"Well, if Freddie and Jackson are right about the prints on the knife belonging to a woman, it would have to be either Rosaline or Roxanne, right?"

"Or Chef Claire," Josie said.

"No, I can't see her as a killer. Can you?"

"Why not?"

"She just seemed like such a nice person," I said.

"Maybe she had a good reason. Maybe Marge's warm and engaging personality finally rubbed her the wrong way."

"I guess anything's possible," I said, shrugging. "But to do that to another person? A knife in the neck." I shuddered again at what we'd discovered in the kitchen.

The office door opened, and Jackson entered. He looked more worn out than us.

"Ladies," he said, removing his hat and sitting down in a chair in front of the desk. "How goes the war?"

"I think we should be asking you that question," I said. "What are you doing here? You get a match on our prints?"

"Geez, Suzy," he said, shaking his head. "Let it go, okay? I swear, sometimes you sound just like your mother."

"What did you say?" I said, almost coming off the couch.

Josie found Jackson's remark particularly funny and laughed loud enough to wake Chloe up. She looked around the room, gave us a quick wag of her tail, then resumed her nap.

"That was a cruel thing to say, Jackson," I said, pouting. "You take that back."

"Take it back? What are you, three?"

"Okay, guys," Josie said. "Let it go. It's been a long day for everybody."

132

I forced myself to calm down and nodded.

"Sorry, Jackson. It's no excuse, but I'm a little on edge."

"Forget it," he said, dismissing the need for an apology with a quick wave.

"So where are you at?" Josie said.

"Well, we tracked down the Chief Operating Officer, Rosaline, and didn't get a match on her prints. And her alibi checked out. Alice stopped by the Water's Edge for a drink after work - the poor kid probably needed one. I don't think this is what she was expecting when she heard she got an internship working on the River all summer. Alice ran into the girlfriend at the bar. Roxanne had been there all afternoon, and there's no way she could have been at the island when Mrs. Crawford bought the farm. But we ran her prints, *per the procedure*." Jackson raised an eyebrow in my direction, and I stuck my tongue out at him.

"Real mature, Suzy," he said, laughing. "Roxanne's prints didn't match either."

"That leaves Chef Claire," Josie said.

"Yeah. Or some unidentified intruder."

"That's a pretty remote place for someone to show up in the middle of the day, isn't it?" I said.

"You would think so," Jackson said. "Unless somebody had been watching the island to get a feel for who was there and when they were coming and going."

"So what's the story with Chef Claire?" Josie said.

"That's what I'd like to know," Jackson said. "She's disappeared."

"Interesting," Josie said. "A runner?"

"We're not sure," he said. "I'm not even sure how she got off the island. All the boats were in the boathouse except for the one the gardener

133

used to run some errands. But he came back while we were all there this afternoon. He says he was alone on the boat the whole time he was away."

"He was," I said. "At least when we saw him."

"When did you see him?"

"Just before we headed over to the island," I said, glancing at Josie.

"You saw him? Why didn't you tell me that earlier when I was interviewing you?"

"You didn't ask," I said, shrugging. "And at the time it didn't seem relevant."

"Suzy, while I appreciate your boundless energy and rather unique detective skills, I think you should leave it up to me to decide what's relevant," he said, scowling at me.

"Next time, ask the question," I snapped.

"Okay, guys, enough," Josie said. "For what it's worth, Jackson, I don't think she was on the boat when we saw Carl earlier. But they were dating."

"What? How the heck do you know that?" Jackson said.

"We've been busy while you were away at your conference," Josie said.

Jackson exhaled and stared up at the ceiling. I would have thought that our hard work and providing new information that could help solve the case would make his job a bit easier. Apparently, we were going to have to agree to disagree on that one.

"Even if she wasn't on the boat when you ran into him, it doesn't mean he hadn't already dropped her off someplace else. Or she got on another boat."

"If she got on a different boat, she could be anywhere," Josie said.

"Yeah. That's why the state police are monitoring her credit cards for activity. If she uses them, we'll know straight away."

"I don't think she did it," I said.

134

"Why is that?" Jackson said, giving me his full attention.

"Because I had dinner with her."

"Well, stop the presses," Jackson said laughing. "You've cracked the case. You had dinner with her? That's it?"

"It was enough. And I don't think I like your attitude, Jackson," I said, glaring at him. "Chef Claire has a gentle soul. And she was the only one on the island who showed the least bit of concern for Chloe."

"So she's a dog lover," Jackson said. "As you know, I appreciate that quality in people, but that's probably not going to be enough to clear her, Suzy."

"If anything, given what she knows about the different players over there and what's going on, if you'd asked me who might be the next person killed, I would have said her."

"What was Rosaline's alibi?" Josie said, grabbing a handful of candy from the jar on the desk.

"It turns out Rosaline has a thing going on with Mrs. Crawford's financial advisor," Jackson said.

"Jerry the Lawyer?" Josie said, glancing at me.

"Yeah, I think that's his name," Jackson said, checking his notebook. "You know him?"

"Yes, we've met," Josie said. "And Suzy's even been on two dates with him."

"Really?" Jackson said.

I glared at Josie. This day was getting worse by the minute. I looked at Jackson.

"Actually, it was only one and a half," I whispered.

"Well, apparently he's been fishing in more than one pond."

"He has not been fishing in my pond, Jackson," I said.

"So far he's just been casting into the shallows," Josie said.

135

"That's enough, Josie," I snapped. "And that's a crude expression, Jackson."

"I could use a more graphic description if you like. Rosaline told us they were holed up all afternoon at the Twin Pines Motel. Jerry confirmed it, as did the motel. The manager said they were making quite the racket. He went into great detail if you want to hear all about it."

"No, we don't," I said.

"Speak for yourself," Josie said, laughing.

I glared at her again and turned up the intensity. I think she got the message, but we'll see. I wasn't sure what I felt about the news of Jerry and Rosaline being an item. Before I had a chance to think it through, Jackson's phone buzzed.

"This is Jackson," he said. "I see... That's good. Well done... Interesting. I'll be right down."

Jackson put his phone away and stood up.

"That was Alice. She got a call from the state police. They found the chef at the Island Towers. She checked in this afternoon. They brought her to the station, checked the prints and got a perfect match."

"Wow," Josie said.

"I don't believe it," I said.

"There's more," Jackson said. "Guess who got fired by Mrs. Crawford this morning?"

"Uh-oh," Josie said. "Motive and opportunity all neatly tied up in a bow."

"They certainly are," he said. "Look, I need to get down to the station. We'll be keeping the chef tonight, and in the morning the state police will come and get her. Do you mind keeping Sluggo one more night? I don't think I'm going to be able to spend any time with him tonight."

136

"That's fine," I said. My mind was going a thousand miles an hour in a hundred different directions. "I'd like to talk to her."

"Why?" Jackson said, pausing at the door.

"Because she's probably scared to death. And I think she might be more willing to talk with us instead of a bunch of cops."

"She's probably already lawyered up. That is if she knows what's good for her."

"I'd like to give it a shot," I said, approaching him. "It can't hurt anything."

"Well, it's not normal procedure," Jackson said.

"Jackson, if you use that term again, I swear, I'm going to punch you in the nose."

"You're threatening an officer of the law?" He couldn't help laughing. "And I've even got a witness."

"No, you don't," Josie said.

Jackson returned my stare then nodded.

"Okay, give me an hour before you swing by the station."

"Thanks, Jackson. I owe you one," I said.

"Now that I think about it, I probably should have used this opportunity as a way to extort a dinner date from Josie."

"Yeah, probably," Josie said, smiling at Jackson then winking at me.

"But I missed my chance, right?"

"You certainly did," Josie said as her smile widened. "But I'll see you in an hour."

Chapter 23

The stone and ivy-clad exterior of the Clay Bay police station, like the rest of our town, appears quaint and serene. In fact, if it wasn't for the fact that it contained a handful of jail cells inside its walls, you might even call it inviting. Josie and I entered and waved hello to Jackson who was sitting at the front desk talking on the phone. We waited until he finished, then he escorted us through a thick door into the area that contained three small cells painted an obnoxious hospital green. It was the first time either Josie or I had seen the area and judging from the expression on her face, which I'm sure was the same as mine, once was more than enough.

Cross that one off the bucket list.

Chef Claire was sitting quietly on her bunk with her hands folded in her lap. People always talk about the look of a killer. Their eyes, their overall demeanor, or something in their makeup that tips you off that they are guilty. Or a face so devoid of expression, it was impossible to get any read on the person. I didn't get either of those reading Chef Claire's face. The only look she seemed to have was one of confusion. Jackson placed two small plastic chairs in front of the cell and left us alone. We sat down, and Chef Claire shifted on the bunk until she was directly facing us, a mere four feet away.

"Hi," I said.

Not a great opener, but it was all I had.

"Hi, Suzy," she said, then looked at Josie. "Your name's Josie, right?"

"Yes. Hi, Chef Claire," Josie said.

"Geez, I guess I didn't get a good look at you at dinner the other night," Chef Claire. "Excuse me for saying this, but you're incredibly beautiful."

138

"Thanks," Josie said, embarrassed by the compliment considering the circumstances of why we were there.

I shook my head in disbelief. Apparently, even incarceration wasn't enough to put a damper on the Josie admiration society.

"Okay, guys," I said, "Before this turns into one of those women in prison movies, let's try to focus. Jackson didn't give us a lot of time."

Both Josie and Chef Claire laughed. I reviewed the list of questions I'd jotted down in the car on the way over and launched right in.

"Would you mind going over what happened this morning?" I said, pencil poised at the ready.

She thought about it briefly, then shrugged. "Nothing out of the ordinary. I got up around seven and made the coffee and started breakfast."

"What was on the menu?" Josie said.

"What difference does that make?" I said, glancing over at her.

"You never know. It might be relevant," Josie said.

"French toast with fresh blueberries," Chef said.

"Yum. Inside the batter or sprinkled on top?"

"Oh, definitely in the batter," Chef Claire said. "When they're part of the batter, the berries become part of the dish and not just something tossed on top at the end."

"I saw that on a cooking show and was wondering if it made a difference," Josie said.

"Absolutely. And I like to crush the berries with a fork first. It totally releases the flavor. You should give it a try," Chef Claire said, nodding.

I stared in disbelief at both of them.

"Really? We're going to spend our time talking about French toast?"

"Sorry," Josie said. "It just sounds delicious."

139

"And I made bacon wrapped sausage links and some fresh rolls," Chef Claire said, glancing at me. "They're the same roll I use for the chili dogs you had the other night."

I remembered the rolls. They were impossible to forget. Despite my desire to get on with the conversation, I felt my stomach growl. I hadn't eaten since the turkey club in the boat.

"It was a carb-heavy meal, but that's what they wanted," Chef Claire said. Then she looked down at the floor. "Not that any of that matters."

"Did Mrs. Crawford eat breakfast?" I said.

"Sure. Like a horse. She had four pieces of French toast and half a plate of the sausages," Chef Claire said.

"And when was this?" I said.

"Right before the witch fired me. That would have been somewhere around nine o'clock."

"I thought she was offering you a position at one of her resort properties," I said, remembering our dinner conversation.

"So did I."

"Did she give you a reason?" I said.

"Yeah, she did. But it wasn't a very good one. It was something about me crossing the line. She was pretty angry when she came down for breakfast, and then I saw her check a message on her phone, and it went even further downhill after that."

"Do you know what the message was?" I said.

"No, when you work for people like Marge, you learn early in your career not to ask many questions. Especially anything that might be personal business."

"So how did it all go down?" I said, leaning forward in my chair.

"How did it *go down*?" Josie said, snorting. "I told you that you've been watching too many cop shows."

140

"Well, excuse me," I said, glaring at her before continuing. "What did she say when she fired you?"

"It was odd," Chef Claire said. "She and I were the only ones at breakfast, so we decided to sit at the island in the kitchen. You know, the same place we had dinner."

I nodded.

"Right after she received the message on her phone, she grabbed her fourth piece of French toast, and I asked her if she would like some more maple syrup and she just snapped. That's when she made the crossing the line comment. Then she said I was fired and had an hour to get off the island."

"Just like that?" Josie said.

"Yup. That was it," Chef Claire said. "But I think I've figured out what the crossing the line remark referred to."

"Something about the maple syrup, right?" I said.

Chef Claire stared at me dumbfounded.

"What?"

"Sorry, I didn't mean to interrupt," I said, embarrassed. "Please continue."

"Smooth," Josie whispered.

"This is a bit hard to say," Chef Claire said, wringing her hands in her lap. "But I think Marge found out that Carl and I had been...well, you know." She fell silent and again stared down at the floor.

"Why would she care if you and Carl saw each other?" I said, then the lightbulb went off. "Really? Marge and Carl?"

"Apparently," Chef Claire said.

"Man, he's a busy guy," Josie whispered. "I'm surprised the lawn looks as good as it does."

"Did you know about him and Marge?"

141

"No, not until the other night."

"When you were..." I said. I recoiled when Josie kicked me under the chair.

Take a breath, Suzy. Good things and good information come to those who wait. Get it together.

"When I was what?" Chef Claire said.

"When you were simply *devastated* to find out about the two of them," I said, pleased with my recovery.

I heard Josie suppress a snort but ignored her.

"I was at Carl's house the other night. I cooked dinner for him."

"What did you make?" Now it was Josie's turn to be embarrassed. "Just curious. I'm always on the lookout for new recipes."

"It was a chicken penne in a brandy cream sauce."

"I knew I smelled cognac," Josie whispered.

"And that was when Carl told you about him and Marge?" I said.

Chef Claire laughed.

"No, Carl would never be the bearer of bad news on an empty stomach. He waited until we ate and...well, you know."

"Why do you think he told you?" Josie said.

"Because I caught him in a lie," Chef Claire said.

"About Marge?" I said.

"No, about the others."

"The others?" I said.

"Sure. Rosaline, Roxanne, a local real estate agent, a couple of waitresses. I could go on, but you get the idea."

"How did you learn about Rosaline and Roxanne?" I said, seizing the opportunity to move the conversation back to the main question of who killed who.

Chef Claire smiled.

142

"That's the beauty of being part of the house staff. I was always there, but at the same time, it was like I was never there. You hear things."

"And it bothered you?" Josie said.

"What? The fact that Carl was seeing other women? Not in the least. I just hate being lied to."

"So you and Carl weren't in a committed relationship?" I said.

For some reason, my question cracked her up. I waited until she stopped laughing and composed herself.

"Relationship?" Chef Claire said. "With Carl? Have you spent any time talking to him? After a half hour of listening to him drone on about the appropriate nitrogen levels for dirt and the blooming patterns of Azaleas, I always wanted to poke my eardrums out with a fork. Fortunately, Carl has other talents. And being stuck on that island all summer, my options were somewhat limited."

"I see," I said.

"So after Marge fired you, what happened next?" Josie said.

"I did what she told me to do. I packed my stuff and left the island."

"Did Carl take you in the boat?" I said.

"No, I haven't spoken to him since the other night," Chef Claire said. "In fact, I didn't even see him around the island before I left."

"But all the boat slips were full," I said slowly, hoping I hadn't just caught her in a lie. I really wanted her to be innocent.

"Yeah, they were," she said, nodding. "I took my boat."

"Your boat?" Josie said.

"Yeah, when I got here at the start of the summer, I thought it would be fun to have a boat of my own to tool around in on my day off. I've never lived near a body of water like this and I wanted to learn how to drive a boat," she said, staring off and apparently recalling some fond memories. "It's a little sixteen-foot aluminum boat with a thirty-five horsepower

143

outboard. It's a lot of fun. But when I showed up for work on my first day, Mr. Crawford took one look at it and said it was an *embarrassment to the watercraft industry* and made me keep it in the boathouse out of sight."

"But where was it?" I said, trying to picture the layout of the boathouse.

"It was up," Chef Claire said. "Above the slips, there's extra storage space. They have an automated hoist system for getting boats in and out of the water. Every time I wanted to use it, I had to lower the boat into the water. And when I returned I had to take it out of the water and get it out of sight. If you never looked up at the ceiling of the boathouse, you wouldn't know it was even there."

"I never noticed," I said, shaking my head.

"Me neither," Josie said.

"Exactly," Chef Claire said. "And that was just the way Mr. Crawford wanted it."

"I guess we can cross that one off the list," I said.

"What?"

"Oh, nothing," I said. "I'm just talking to myself."

"I do it all the time," Chef Claire said. "It's a nice break in the day."

I knew I liked this woman for a reason.

"After I left the island, I decided to check into the Island Towers for a couple of days until I got my last check. And I needed a few days to figure out what I'm going to do next. I was taking a nap when the cops showed up and brought me in. Two hours later, they put me in here. And I hear that tomorrow I'm going to be moved to a *more secure* location."

"They found your prints on the knife," I said.

"So they tell me," Chef Claire said.

"How do you explain that?" I said, leaning forward in my chair. Finally, I was doing some real detective work.

144

"I'm a chef. They're my work knives," she said. "How do you think they got there?"

Wow. I touched a sore spot with that one. Either she was on the defensive, or she thought it was the stupidest question she'd ever heard. Actually, when I replayed it in my head, it was kind of a dumb question.

"So you didn't kill her?" I said.

"Of course not," she snapped. "I just told you I left the island, and when I left she was still in the kitchen stuffing chocolate croissants down her gullet."

"You made chocolate croissants, too?" Josie said.

I looked at Josie, and for a moment I thought I noticed a trace of drool on her lips.

"Yeah, I put a piece of dark chocolate and a dollop of fresh whipped cream in each one before I bake them off. They're incredible."

"Guys, please," I said. "Enough with the food. Can we stick with what's important?"

"In what world aren't chocolate croissants important?" Chef Claire said.

"Yeah," Josie said, glaring back at me. "What she said."

Despite the fact that the woman on the other side of the bars was facing murder charges, all three of us laughed.

"It's obvious I'm being set up here," Chef Claire said.

"But by who?" I said.

"I don't know. But I don't think it's anyone with a vendetta against me. I think I'm being set up because whoever killed Marge figured out a way to make me an easy target and keep the focus off of them."

"Your prints on the knife are going to a major problem," I said.

"Maybe," she said.

"What do you mean, maybe?"

145

"Think about it," Chef Claire said. "It doesn't add up."

Before she could continue, the door opened, and Jackson stepped inside the cell area.

"Don't mean to interrupt, but we need to wrap this up," he said. "I've already pushed the envelope just by letting you in here."

"Just a few more minutes, Jackson," I said.

"No," he said with a firm shake of his head. "You're done."

"Please," Josie said.

"No, not even for a dinner date," he said, ending the conversation.

We both stood, and I looked at Chef Claire who was sitting back down with the same confused look she'd had when we first came in.

"We'll be in touch," I said. "Do you need anything?"

"No, I'm fine," she said. "My lawyer will have to take it from here."

Out of words that might offer condolences or encouragement, I waved goodbye and followed Josie and Jackson back into the main area of the jail.

"She didn't do it, Jackson," I said.

"Suzy, I hate to say this, but I've got a motive, opportunity, and a set of prints that say otherwise."

"You're wrong, Jackson." I felt my throat constrict, and my voice went up an octave as the severity of Chef Claire's situation finally hit home with me. Up until that moment, I'd been selfish; caught up in the events and the thrill of trying to put the pieces of the puzzle together. Now, the consequences of the two murders were unfolding. Unfortunately, when they had opened up, they'd landed right in Chef Claire's lap.

"She's not a killer, Jackson," Josie said, patting my arm.

That's the thing about my best friend. Josie always comes through when I need her. I recovered a bit of my composure and felt somewhat chuffed with pride that I'd guided the conversation to the point where Josie had seen and heard enough to be convinced that Chef Claire was innocent.

146

Of course, it could have been the blueberry French toast and chocolate croissants that changed her mind.

Chapter 24

I scanned the menu, decided on a cheeseburger with a side of onion rings, and closed the menu. I sipped my coffee and looked across the table at Josie who was carefully studying her options. She flipped to the next page of the menu and took a sip of coffee without looking up. Impressed by her focus and attention to detail I wondered if I'd missed something so I changed my mind for the third time and opened my menu and started over.

"I'm worried," I said, scanning the appetizers.

"That I'll never be able to make a decision, and you'll end up starving to death right at this table?"

"Well, yeah, there is that," I said, changing my mind to the chicken pot pie with a side of stuffed mushrooms. "But I was referring to Chef Claire."

The mention of her name caused Josie to close her menu and look up. She nodded and took another sip of coffee.

"Yeah, it's not good," she said. "A high-powered CEO and island owner, along with his socialite ex-wife get killed on the River. Jackson must be under a lot of pressure to get this thing resolved. I'm sure there are a lot of people worried about the impact a couple of murders could have on tourism."

"Given the way the world is going these days, tourism will probably go up."

Josie laughed, then waved at our waitress. "Yeah, you're probably right."

The waitress, a young college student, named Mandy, arrived brandishing an iPad. The days of the traditional diner were rapidly disappearing but the Last Stop of the Night was doing its best to hold on against the chains and fast food franchises. But they had made the concession to technology, and since they'd gone electronic with their ordering system, I had to admit that the service had gotten faster and more accurate.

"Hi, folks," Mandy said. "Isn't it a little late for you two to be out?"

"Hey, we're not that old," Josie said. "We can hang with the young crowd when we want to."

"Yeah," I said, playing along. "Just last week I stayed up until almost midnight two nights in a row."

"I'll call TMZ to be on the lookout," Mandy said. "What can I get you?"

"Now that I think about it, can I get breakfast?" I said. "I have a sudden urge for French Toast."

"Oh, that sounds good," Josie said.

"Normally, I'd say yes," Mandy said. "But Johnny's in a really bad mood tonight, and he said no breakfast orders. Apparently, he went to Saratoga yesterday and lost big at the track and then had a fight with his wife." She shrugged her condolences. "Sorry."

"Dang," I said. "Okay, I'll have the pot pie with a side of the stuffed mushrooms."

"I'll have an order of the stuffed mushrooms as well. And fried chicken, onion rings, and a slice of blueberry pie with a scoop of vanilla for dessert."

Mandy, well-versed in Josie's prodigious eating abilities, didn't bat an eye. She typed in our orders, refilled our coffees, and headed off. I looked around the diner that was busy with late night revelers looking to end their evening with a full stomach to help minimize tomorrow morning's hangover.

"You know, Clay Bay could use another year round place to eat," I said.

149

"Yeah, it could. I've got this menu memorized. I don't know why I even bother to look at it when we come in."

"We need to get a look at that knife," I whispered as I leaned forward.

"Geez, Suzy. I don't know if that's such a good idea," Josie said, shaking her head. "You heard Jackson. Jackson's already nervous about us sticking our nose in where it doesn't belong."

"Hey, if it hadn't been for us, they might not have even *found* the bodies," I snapped.

Josie glared at me with a puzzled expression on her face.

"Why are you yelling at me?"

"I'm sorry," I said. "But the whole situation is so unfair. And I have a pretty good feeling that the knife will tell us something."

"We need to be careful, Suzy. This isn't like the time we were trying to figure out who was setting fire to the neighbor's vegetable garden. This is serious stuff. And an obstruction of justice charge is not something we want to be dealing with."

"Let me ask you this, if Chef Claire is convicted, do you think that justice will have been served?"

"No, I don't," Josie said, patting my hand. "Okay, I'll talk with Freddie and see if he's willing to let us take a look at the knife."

"Good," I said. "Freddie won't say no to you."

"Can I at least eat first?" Josie said, watching Mandy approach carrying stuffed mushrooms piled high on both plates.

"Sure. We need to keep our strength up. We're in this thing for the long haul."

Mandy set the plates down, checked to see if we needed anything else, then left the table. We spent the next few minutes in silence as we began our attack on the mushrooms. They didn't stand a chance. I came up for air first

150

and took a long sip of water and wiped my mouth. A couple in a booth at the back of the diner caught my eye.

"Oh, that's interesting," I said. "I can't believe I didn't see them sitting there earlier."

"Who is it?" Josie said, more out of politeness than interest.

"Jerry the Lawyer and his girlfriend."

"Rosaline?" she said, craning her neck towards the back of the diner.

"The very one," I said. "I'm going to go have a word with them."

"Suzy, nothing good can come from that conversation," Josie said, returning to her rapidly dwindling stack of mushrooms.

"You're probably right." I slid my way out of the booth and stood up. "But I can't help myself."

"Knock yourself out," Josie said through a mouthful of mushroom.

As I approached their booth, Rosaline saw me first. Judging by her expression, I don't think she was delighted to see me. Jerry had his back to me, and he noticed the look on Rosaline's face then turned around. He wasn't happy to see me.

"Hi, folks," I said, forcing a smile.

"Hi," Rosaline said. Her voice was flat, and it looked like she'd been crying.

"Suzy," Jerry said, his face flushed. "It's nice to see you."

"Oh, I doubt that," I said, widening my smile.

"Would you care to join us?" he said, sliding over in the booth.

Rosaline blanched. "I don't think that's a good-"

"Thanks," I said, sliding into the booth. "I'd be delighted."

Rosaline set her fork down and pushed her plate away, then sat back in the booth and folded her arms. She glared at me. I assumed that Jerry had divulged the fact that we'd been out one and a half times.

"Crazy day, huh?" I said.

151

"Yeah, it sure was," Jerry said to his plate.

"What do you want?" Rosaline said.

"Nothing. I just wanted to confirm the rumor about you two before the next time Jerry calls and asks me out."

"What rumor?" Rosaline said.

"The rumor that you two spent the afternoon at the Twin Pines Motel. The manager said you made quite a racket."

"So we get loud from time to time," Rosaline said. "The last time I checked, that wasn't against the law."

"No, I'm sure it's not," I said, now wondering why I'd decided to sit down in the first place.

Note to self. When in doubt, listen to Josie.

"Uh, look, Suzy," Jerry said. "I probably should have said something to you about Rosaline."

"Why?" I said. "It was just dinner."

Rosaline snorted. I couldn't tell if it was directed at Jerry or me. Regardless, judging from the look on her face and his reaction, he was fully expecting to bear the brunt. I decided on a new topic of conversation.

"So, what are you going to do now, Rosaline?" I said.

"Actually, we were just talking about that," Jerry said.

"Not that it's any of your business," Rosaline said. "But I'm probably going to have to go into hiding until the police figure out who Chef Claire is working for."

Startled by the response, I sat back in the booth and stared at Rosaline.

"What do you mean who she's working for?" I said, glancing at Jerry who continued to pick half-heartedly at his mac and cheese.

"This is obviously an attempt to destabilize the Crawford Candy Company. And now that Mr. Crawford and the potential heir to the operation are dead, as Jackson Operating Officer, it's only logical to assume that I'm the next target on their list."

"Hmmm," I said.

I was using a technique I'd learned over the years watching detective shows. When in doubt, say something sage. Hmmm was the best I could come up with on short notice.

"You said Mrs. Crawford was the potential heir. I would have thought that would have been worked out in their divorce settlement."

Rosaline transitioned into exasperated and exhaled loudly. She gave Jerry a *'You're so going to pay for this'* look, then refocused on me.

"It's a complicated situation," Rosaline said. "Lots of legal questions, shareholder concerns, and a host of other issues I'm sure you wouldn't be interested in." And then she whispered, just loud enough for me to hear. "Or understand."

Okay, so that's the way you want to play it. She's going to pay for that crack.

"Of course," I said, nodding. "But how will you continue doing your job if you have to go into hiding?"

"I'll figure something out," Rosaline said, her eyes narrowed. "I always do."

"Yes," I said. "I'm sure you do."

"Executives have to adapt if they expect to survive," she said. "Mr. Crawford taught me that lesson a long time ago."

"That's why I spend my day surrounded by dogs," I said, laughing. "And by the way, Chloe is doing great. She's growing like a weed."

"Good for her," Rosaline said, flatly.

"I guess I should get going," I said, sliding out of the booth. "There's a chicken pot pie over there with my name on it. But if I don't get there soon, I'm sure Josie won't be shy about claiming it."

153

"Oh, yes," Rosaline said, glancing down the rows of booths. "The queen bee beauty queen of Clay Bay. The big fish. But such a small pond."

I glared down at Rosaline.

"Josie would be the big fish in whatever size pond she decided to swim in."

"I seriously doubt that," Rosaline said. "But if that helps make you happy with whatever limited life choices you've both made, go for it."

"I guess there's only room for one queen bee, huh?"

"It's nice to see you've been paying attention," she said, reaching across the table to grab Jerry's hand.

"I imagine that's a lesson you learned from Mrs. Crawford."

"Not really," Rosaline said, shrugging. "I learned that long before I met her." Her eyes welled with tears. "But I'm sure there were many things I could have learned from Marge if we'd gotten the chance to work together. Now, I'm afraid we'll never know."

Out of words and on the verge of feeling sympathy for her, I waved goodbye and walked back to the booth.

"How'd it go?" Josie said through a bite of an onion ring.

I picked up my fork and poked a couple of holes in the crust to release the steam trapped inside my chicken pot pie. At least it was still hot. I guess the evening wasn't a total disaster.

"Not well. You were right."

"You're welcome," she said.

We both glanced up at the same time. Jerry was hovering by our booth.

"I need to talk with you," he said.

"Why?" I said, sliding a piece of chicken into my mouth.

"I need to explain a few things," he said, glancing back at his booth.

"I don't think Rosaline would approve," I said.

"Oh, there's no doubt about that," he said. "But that doesn't matter at the moment. Can I take you to dinner tomorrow night?"

"No, dinner is, so to speak, off the table at the moment," I said, shaking my head.

"You need to give me a chance to explain," Jerry said, his eyes pleading.

"No, I don't think I do," I said, taking another bite.

"How's the pot pie?" Josie said.

"It's delicious. Want a bite?"

"No, thanks. I'm waiting for my dessert," Josie said.

"C'mon, Suzy. Are you going to make me beg?" Jerry said.

"That would probably be a good start," Josie said.

"I think talking will help," Jerry said.

"Help who?" I said, finally looking up at him.

"Us... You... Me? Gee, I don't know," he said, managing a small laugh.

The laugh worked, and I thought for a moment before nodding my head.

"Okay," I said. "But no dinner. You can buy me breakfast tomorrow. I'll meet you at nine at the Café."

"That's great," he said, beaming. "I'll see you there. Goodnight, Josie."

We both watched him walk away as Mandy delivered Josie's blueberry pie and ice cream. Josie started working on it immediately. I resumed eating my dinner.

"He is cute," Josie said, wiping ice cream off her mouth.

"Yeah. And smart. Pity he has a girlfriend."

"And hates dogs," Josie said. "Rosaline seems like a strange choice for him, don't you think?"

155

"No, I can see it," I said. "They're both corporate types, and they have a tendency to stick with their own kind, right?"

"I guess," Josie said. "By the way, good job making him work as hard as you did. And nice touch on doing it over breakfast."

"Thanks. I thought you'd appreciate that."

"You're going to have the French toast, aren't you?"

"I certainly am."

"I like the way you think."

Chapter 25

It was raining hard the next morning. Luckily I found a parking spot right outside the Café and only got mildly drenched covering the twenty feet from my car to the entrance. I walked inside, said hello to the hostess, and found Jerry sitting on a small bench near the cash register.

"Good morning," he said, staring intensely at me.

"What is it?" I said, touching my hair, then glancing down at myself.

In my race to get here on time, without the assistance of morning coffee, had I forgotten to do something important? Perhaps I'd neglected to put on makeup.? Or my pants. I glanced in the mirror behind the cash register, and everything seemed to be in order. I turned back to Jerry who continued to stare at me. It was officially getting on my nerves.

"Why are you staring at me?"

"I'm sorry," he said. "It's just that not many women could look as beautiful coming in out of the rain."

"Geez, Jerry," I said. "Don't start with that nonsense. I haven't even had coffee yet. Besides, it's a lie, and we both know it."

"I'm not lying," Jerry said, following the laughing hostess to our table.

I sat down and accepted the menu from the hostess. She also handed me a small towel.

"I'm not sure if you want this, Suzy," she said, still chuckling. "You might ruin the overall look."

"You'll get yours, Abby," I said, snatching the towel from her hand. "Just you wait."

She laughed and headed back toward the entrance. I wiped my face, blotted at my hair, then gave up and tossed the towel on the table. Our waitress approached carrying two mugs and a pot of coffee.

"Hi, Eunice," I said smiling up at the woman who'd worked at the Café longer than I've been alive.

"How are you doing, Suzy? Would you both like coffee?"

We nodded yes, and she poured then left to give us time to decide on our order. I didn't need it. I knew exactly what I wanted. I added milk to my coffee and took a sip. I nodded, took a deep breath, and decided, even though my morning caffeine levels were dangerously low, I was ready to do battle.

"So, you mentioned something about an explanation. What do you have to tell me?"

"Getting right to it, huh?" Jerry said, putting down his menu. "You sure you wouldn't like to eat first?"

"I'm not much of a multitasker, but I'm sure I can handle talking and eating at the same time," I said, drumming my fingers on the table. "And I have a ton of work to take care of today."

That was true. I did. This detective stuff, especially for amateurs like me, is a real time sucker.

"Okay," he said. "First, I guess I should apologize."

"What exactly are you apologizing for, Jerry?"

Wow. I caught him right between the eyes with that one. He looked at me, blinked, and then stared out the window at the rain. I grew even more annoyed with him. I mean, really. The guy had all night to come up with an answer for that one. It should have been a layup.

"I'm sorry for not being *clearer* with you at dinner the other night," he said.

"Clearer?"

"Yes," he said. "I think that's the right word. I should have been more forthcoming about my *situation* with Rosaline."

"By situation, do you mean the part about how you like to spend your afternoons in cheap roadside motels?"

"I guess that's part of it," he said, running a hand through his hair.

I was on a roll this morning. Only two sips of coffee and I already had him on the ropes.

"I would have thought that you'd be apologizing to Rosaline," I said, reloading caffeine. "She was the one you were trying to cheat on."

"Yeah, about that," he said. "Rosaline and I have a connection that's hard to explain."

"I bet."

I thought about asking him if their *connection* including her getting busy with Carl the Gardener. But if he didn't know about Rosaline and Carl, he might start obsessing about that and lose his ability to focus on anything else.

The waitress arrived. I ordered French toast and sausage and sat back in my chair with my arms folded across my chest. Jerry fumbled through the menu and eventually decided on an omelet with sourdough toast. We handed the menus to the waitress, and she topped off our coffee and left.

"You should have ordered the French toast," I said. "It's really good here."

"I'm not a big fan," he said, again staring out the window at the rain that continued to pound.

"Who doesn't like French toast?"

"It's not that. The toast is fine. It's the maple syrup I don't like."

"Too sweet?"

"Yeah, that must be it. I loved it when I was a kid, but my taste buds changed at some point. And now that the Crawford's were both found drenched in it when they got killed, it's definitely off my list."

"That's right," I said. "I almost forgot. You're down a client."

"That's not a problem. I was kind of glad to see her go. But not the way she did." Jerry shrugged and sipped his coffee. He started humming a children's ditty that sounded familiar. I finally remembered it. *The Wheels on the Bus*. I thought it was an odd choice for a grown man, but I guess we all have our baggage to deal with. I listened to him hum it twice as he stared out the window, then he stopped and looked at me.

"I hope we can get past this," he said.

"Jerry, I hate to tell you this, but there is no we. There never was."

I fell silent and then I heard the children's ditty running through my head. Great. Thanks for sharing that with me, Jerry.

"But you did feel something during dinner, right? I know I did."

"Maybe," I conceded. "But that was before I found out you're in a relationship."

"It's not that kind of a relationship."

"Jerry, if it includes moaning in roadside motels in the middle of the afternoon, as far as I'm concerned, it's that kind of relationship. And if you would lie to Rosaline, then you'd probably lie to me, too. That's the way it always seems to work."

"Yeah, I can understand why you'd feel that way."

He gave me his best hound dog expression. I stared back at it. Then he tried a smile. Better, but not good enough to get my mind off my undelivered breakfast. I glanced at the kitchen. Not a piece of French toast in sight. So I decided to put the time to good use. And anything was better than talking about the dreaded *we*.

"Josie and I had an interesting visit from Mrs. Crawford the other day."

160

"Really?" he said, taking his eyes off the rain to look at me. "Most of my time with Marge was anything but interesting."

"She was looking for a key," I said.

"A key? And she thought you had it?"

"Actually, she thought Chloe could have swallowed it."

"I guess a dog could be stupid enough to do something like that."

Then he realized what he'd said and who he'd said it to and blanched.

"I didn't mean that," he said. "I'm sorry."

I glared at him. The final vestige of his chances for a comeback vaporized.

"Look, Suzy, I take that back," he said, backpedaling as fast as his little legs could carry him. Then he realized it was futile. "Ah, forget it." He leaned back in his chair and now that he realized he'd completely blown his chances with me, he seemed to relax. "So, did the dog eat it?"

"No. Did Mrs. Crawford ever mention that she was looking for a key?"

"Not to me," he said. "But Rosaline figured out that she was looking for something. She cleaned the entire house by herself. That's something psychologists would call an *out of character behavioral pattern*." He frowned, deep in thought. "I think that's the term."

"What do you think she was looking for?"

"We're not sure," he said. "My guess is that Marge thought there was some paperwork floating around that might prevent her from gaining control of the Crawford empire. Who knows? Rich people, right?"

"And you were helping her figure out all her options?"

"Yeah, basically," he said.

"Has Rosaline decided where she's going to go?"

"Yeah," he said flatly.

"And?"

"And that has to remain a secret given the danger she might be in."

161

"Are you going with her?" I said, spotting our waitress heading our way.

"Uh, that topic is still, let's say, under consideration."

We both sat back as the waitress slid our plates in front of us.

"We just switched syrups so let me know what you think," she said.

"I'm sure it'll do the trick, Eunice," I said, laughing.

"Yeah, it's not bad," she said. "Mind you, it's not Sugarland Farms, but what is, right?"

I didn't have a clue what she was talking about. Jerry ignored her as he examined his plate.

She topped off our coffee again and waited until she was satisfied we had everything we needed, then left. I reached for the maple syrup container and poured it all over my French toast dusted with powdered sugar. A handful of blueberries were tossed over the top. I made a mental note to have a word with the cook about Chef Claire's blended technique.

"You sure you don't want to try it?" I said.

"No, thanks," Jerry said, shaking his head.

I took a big bite and sighed audibly.

"I bet you wish you could make her moan like that, Jerry."

We both glanced up and saw Rosaline staring down at us. She was drenched, and her eyes were wide and wild.

"You thought you were just going to sneak out with this trollop without me finding out?"

Trollop? If it hadn't been for the French toast, I would have been at her throat. But since she was Jerry's problem, I decided to keep eating and see how he played it.

"Relax, Rosaline," Jerry said, embarrassed. "It's just breakfast."

"So I see," she said, removing her coat and shaking it just hard enough to spray some water on my face. She hung the coat on a nearby hook and sat down.

"I guess I could eat," she said, grabbing a fork from the empty table next to us and taking a bite of Jerry's omelet. Then she picked up a piece of his sourdough toast and glared at me as she chewed. Jerry stared back out the window apparently longing to be outside playing in the rain.

"How's the French toast?" Rosaline said, pointing her fork at my plate.

"It's amazing," I said, resolved not to react and provoke the response I knew she was hoping for. "And I'll have to ask them what brand of maple syrup this is. It's incredible."

"I'll be the judge of that," she said, cutting off a piece of my French toast with her fork. She swirled it in the maple syrup and shoveled it into her mouth. "Yeah, it's okay. But I think it's been stepped on a bit with some extra sugar. So technically, it's not 100% pure maple syrup."

She noticed the confused look on my face and shrugged.

"When you work for the Crawford Candy Company you're forced to become an expert on all sorts of things. Especially the things that go into our candy." She paused to take a quick look outside at the rain still pounding the pavement. "When I was a kid, my parents only allowed one brand in the house."

"Where was that, Rosaline?"

"In a distant land, in another time," she said, helping herself to another bite. "How about you, Suzy? Where did you grow up?"

"Right here in Clay Bay," I said.

"That explains a lot," she said, maintaining her glare.

"Rosaline, please," Jerry said, pushing his plate away.

"I'll deal with you later," she said.

"Yes, I'm sure you will," Jerry said.

163

"You're weak," she said, talking to him, but looking at me.

"So where did you two lovebirds meet?" I said.

"She's funny, Jerry," Rosaline said, chuckling.

Actually, it sounded like a mad cackle, but I wasn't about to go into it with her.

"We connected in New York last year," Rosaline said. "Mrs. Crawford had just resurfaced and was looking for some financial advice. She asked Mr. Crawford to handle it, and Jerry was one of the people we interviewed. He and I just hit it off. Isn't that right, sweetie?"

She squeezed his upper thigh hard. Jerry winced but managed a smile.

"We certainly did, Rosaline," he whispered.

"What can I say?" she said, flashing me a smile. "Jerry knows what gets my motor running. And all the good things that happen when it gets revved up. Don't you, sweetie?"

"I guess," Jerry whispered.

As I watched, it became apparent this wasn't the first time they'd had this conversation. Without a doubt, they were one of the weirdest couples I'd ever met. And I'd definitely dodged a bullet by not getting involved with him. If he was willing to tolerate this level of abuse, Jerry was damaged goods. But not nearly as damaged as the whirling dervish sitting next to me and making short work of my breakfast.

"This is pretty good," she said, chewing with her mouth open.

"Look, I need to run," I said, getting up from my chair.

"Don't let me run you off," Rosaline said.

"It's okay," I said, glancing down at my empty plate. "I have a bunch of dogs who need tending to."

"Be careful, Suzy," Rosaline said, giving me another evil smile. "Try not to get any on you."

"I'm afraid it's too late to worry about that," I said, heading for the exit.

164

Oh, good one. If I'd had a microphone, I would have dropped it. I wanted to sneak a look back to see if my parting shot had hit home with her but kept my eyes focused on the door. I stepped outside into the driving rain. I walked to my car as it poured over my head and shoulders and felt somehow cleansed.

Chapter 26

Around our house, Wednesday is movie night. Actually, in the interest of clarity and full disclosure, Wednesday night is WIJ Night. For the uninitiated, a WIJ is a woman-in-jeopardy movie where the heroine is subjected to constant torment and travails as she tries to deal with whatever challenges are facing her. In tonight's movie, the main character was being stalked by an unknown assailant while trying to convince the police that her friend was being framed for a murder she didn't commit.

For obvious reasons, I related quite strongly to the storyline and was rooting hard for the heroine.

It had poured all day, and it continued into the evening. Outside it was darker than my mood that had turned cranky after breakfast and by the end of the day, had morphed into downright cantankerous.

But it wasn't like I didn't have several good reasons to be in a foul mood. After breakfast, I discovered I had a flat tire. I had my suspicions about how it got that way but no proof. At lunchtime, Chloe had managed to get up on a chair, and then her hind legs to press the button that controlled the automatic door lock system on the condos. We discovered the problem when two dozen dogs were herded by Chloe into the reception area much to the dismay of a nervous Chihuahua and her overbearing owner. After the Chihuahua had shaken violently and then peed on her owner's lap, they left in a huff and vowed never to come back.

That was okay with me. I liked the dog and would miss her; the owner, not so much.

While I was dealing with that mini-crisis, one member of Chloe's herd had discovered my lunch on the counter and before I could get to it, my second meal of the day was devoured by someone other than the intended recipient.

During her lunch break, Josie called Freddie, the county medical examiner, to see if we could swing by to take a look at the knife with Chef Claire's prints on it. But he was out of town investigating a boating accident about twenty miles downriver and wouldn't be back in the office until morning. Then Jackson had called to tell us that Chef Claire had been denied bail and was being transferred to a woman's prison outside of Rochester while she awaited trial.

And just when I'd convinced myself the day couldn't get any worse I slipped and fell in the mud on my walk up the hill from the Inn to the house. Chloe had decided I needed rescuing and joined me in the mud pile. Then she decided that playing in the mud was more fun than her rescue attempt, so she dug and rolled in the wet mess while I struggled to my feet.

Josie laughed until tears rolled down her cheeks, a reaction I found particularly annoying, and if it hadn't been for the meatloaf and mashed potatoes she made for dinner, I probably still wouldn't be speaking to her.

An hour and two baths later, I was finally able to kick back in my sweats with a glass of Pinot Noir and see if the challenges presented to the woman in the WIJ were any match for my own. I stretched out on the couch, and Chloe hopped up and draped herself across my legs.

"No, don't open that door," Josie said to the TV. "Don't go in there, girl."

"I don't think she can hear you, Josie."

Josie laughed and leaned down to pet the snoring Sluggo who was sacked out at her feet.

"It's nice to see you back in the land of the living," she said.

"Yeah, sorry about all that," I said. "Bad day all around."

167

"Yes, it was," she said, staring out the window at the rain that continued to pound down. "I wonder how Chef Claire is doing."

I winced at the thought of being locked up behind bars. Then I noticed headlights heading up the driveway.

"That must be Jackson," I said, peeking through the curtains. "He said he'd swing by on his way home to pick up Sluggo. Just in time, too. Another day with you and he'd never want to leave."

Josie leaned over again and scratched the bulldog's ear. "Wakey, wakey, Sluggo. Daddy's here."

Sluggo snorted in his sleep and rolled over.

We heard a quick knock on the door followed by footsteps.

Normally, I would have gotten up to answer the door and greet a guest. But Jackson was considered family. And family members were expected to fend for themselves.

"Wet clothes stay in the kitchen," I called from the comfort of the couch.

"Way ahead of you," Jackson said.

Moments later he walked into the living room trailed by Freddie.

"Good evening, ladies," Freddie said. "I hope you don't mind that I tagged along. On the phone, it sounded like you were anxious to see me."

Sluggo woke when he heard Jackson's voice and bounded across the room as fast as he could. Which was pretty slow. We watched the reunion play out as Josie poured wine for them. We put the DVR on pause, turned the TV off, and settled into our seats.

"How are you doing, Freddie?" I said.

"I spent all day in a cold driving rain trying to pull two bodies out of a marsh so thick the ducks won't even go in there," he said. "But I've had worse."

168

We watched as he dug through his work bag and removed an evidence box.

"Jackson agreed to let me show you this. But not unless he was in the room when I did it."

"I'm still not sure why I agreed to it," Jackson said.

"Because you can't say no to us, Jackson," Josie said.

"I think I should get a dinner date out of this," he said.

"No," Josie said.

"How come the word no is so easy for you?" Jackson said.

"Practice makes perfect," Josie said.

"Okay, it's in a plastic bag, and it needs to stay there," Freddie said. "You can look, but don't touch the knife. Got it?"

Josie and I nodded and followed him to a table where we huddled around him as he removed the sealed bag from the box and placed it on the table. Josie turned on the light above the table, and we stared down at it. There were blood stains on the blade and whatever powder had been used to locate the fingerprints had worked to perfection. Several clear swirls were all over the handle.

"Okay, that big one near the top of the handle is a thumbprint. It's a partial, but it's definitely hers." Freddie said, using a small flashlight to highlight the print. He carefully repositioned the plastic bag. "And directly underneath that one are three fingers. The pinkie finger wasn't on the knife."

I stared down at the knife and studied the prints. I shook my head, and Josie looked at me.

"What is it?" she said.

"It doesn't make any sense," I said.

"I don't know what to tell you, Suzy," Freddie said. "They're obviously Chef Claire's prints."

"Yes, I'm sure they are," I said, nodding.

169

"Then what's the problem?" Jackson said.

I headed into the kitchen and returned moments later with a similar knife.

"What are you doing, Suzy? There's no need to kill the messenger," Freddie said, laughing as he took a step back in mock fear.

"You're a funny guy, Freddie," I said.

"I try," he said, giving Josie a quick look.

I held the knife in my hand the way you would to chop vegetables and extended my hand forward at a ninety-degree angle.

"The prints indicate that she was holding the knife like this, right?"

"Basically, yes," Freddie said, nodding. "So?"

"So, that's not the way you would hold a knife if you were going to stab somebody in the neck," I said.

"Why not?" Freddie said, staring at the knife.

"Because it's awkward. It's not a natural movement," I said, thrusting the knife back and forth in the air.

"Not for you, maybe," Jackson said. "But for a trained chef with years of experience working with knives, it wouldn't be that hard."

"No, I'm not buying it, Jackson," I said. "When we found the body in the kitchen, the knife was slightly angled down, right?"

"Yes, twelve degrees," Freddie said.

"That means that whoever did it was standing above Mrs. Crawford," I said.

Jackson and Freddie glanced at each other.

"Maybe a little," Freddie said.

"At a minimum, if they were both standing up, Chef Claire would have to have been at least eye to eye."

"Yes," Jackson said. "She would."

170

"Then if I was going to stab someone holding the knife like this, wouldn't it make more sense to go for the stomach. That would be a much easier target."

"Maybe Mrs. Crawford was sitting down," Freddie said. "Chef Claire said they'd eaten breakfast together."

"Yes, but they ate at the kitchen island. You both saw how high those stools are. Chef Claire barely clears five feet in heels. Even if Mrs. Crawford were sitting down when she got stabbed, Chef Claire would have had to strike with an upward motion."

"Maybe Mrs. Crawford was already on the floor," Jackson said, frowning. "Everyone said she'd spent the last couple of days cleaning the house."

"Really, Jackson?" I said. "She was on her knees cleaning the floor in the middle of breakfast?"

"Hey, I'm just thinking out loud here," he snapped. "Who knows? Maybe she dropped her croissant."

"Or maybe Chef Claire was standing on top of the island," Freddie said.

Josie made a noise that sounded like it could have come from Sluggo. Freddie turned to look at her.

"What are you snorting about?" Freddie said.

"She climbed up on the island?" Josie said. "Next, you'll have her swinging in on a chandelier like a pirate."

"Hey, anything's possible," Freddie said. "This is the thanks Jackson and I get for agreeing to show you the knife in the first place? We didn't need to do that. You two do realize that, don't you?"

Nice counterattack, Freddie. Score a point for the ME. Forceful and straight to the point. I realized I needed to calm down and took a few deep breaths.

171

"Look, all I'm saying is that if I were going to stab somebody from behind, I'd hold it like this." I repositioned the knife into my fist and then made a downward stabbing motion. "This is how I'd do it."

"Thanks for the warning," Freddie said.

I laughed and realized that Freddie was starting to grow on me. From the look on Josie's face, it appeared she was thinking along the same lines.

"So how do you explain it, Suzy?" Jackson said.

"The murder weapon was a different knife," I said.

Wow. Thank you, Ms. Subconscious. Where did that come from? But it sounded good, so I decided to stay with it.

"What?" Jackson said.

"Think about it," I said.

I hoped they would. I needed a bit of time to formulate my theory.

"It could have been the same model and brand. But a different knife. Freddie, were the neck wounds torn and jagged?"

"Suzy, take another look at the size of that knife. Of course, they were torn and jagged," Freddie said.

"Is it possible that the first knife was removed and then replaced with Chef Claire's after Mrs. Crawford was killed?

Freddie considered the idea and then slowly nodded. "Yeah, I guess it could have been. If the knives matched and you took the time to position the second knife into the original wound. Yeah, I can go with that as a possibility."

"It's the perfect way to set her up for the murder," I said. "Anybody around the house would know that Chef Claire's prints would be all over her knives."

"But who would do it? Or why?" Freddie said.

"I have no idea," I said, shaking my head. "But I know Chef Claire didn't kill Marge Crawford."

172

"Mrs. Crawford had just fired her that morning. She's the only one with a motive, Suzy," Jackson said.

"The only one we've identified so far. And getting fired is not a motive," I said. "That was a blessing. Chef Claire could get a job anywhere she wanted."

"Maybe," Jackson said. "I don't know, Suzy. It seems like a bit of a stretch. But I have to say it's an intriguing theory."

"Thanks, Jackson."

"How do you suggest we go about proving it?" Jackson said.

"I have no idea."

Chapter 27

I left my office and entered the main reception area and watched Jill simultaneously handle a phone call, a check-in, and process payments for two departing guests and their owners. Sammy was playing traffic cop as a half dozen dogs on leashes made their way in, out, and around the Inn. I felt like a proud mom as I watched them and the rest of the staff perform their duties without a hitch and genuine smiles on their faces. We'd come a long way from the early days when Josie and I were pretty much on our own until we'd gotten established. And now the Inn was a thriving enterprise that was considered an important member of the local community. As I watched the hustle and bustle, I had a thought that it might be a good time to start thinking about taking that long overdue vacation.

Before I had time to ponder possible locations or fantasize about sunny beaches and umbrellas drinks, a cloud of dust coming up the driveway caught my attention. I looked out through the front window and saw my mother climb out of a massive black SUV with tinted windows.

I stepped out onto the front porch and watched her approach. It looked like it must be a golf day and she was wearing an outfit dominated by pink and yellow. It seemed like something a young girl might wear, but like everything she wore it worked for her. She removed her sunglasses as she reached the front steps and then nodded her head at the SUV.

"Well, what do you think?"

"What happened, Mom? Did the Canadian officials impound your Ferrari?"

"Funny, darling," she said, climbing the steps. "No, after watching a couple of video clips that Jackson sent me showing high-speed car crashes, I knew I had to make a decision."

"To act your age, right?"

"My, aren't we on a roll this morning," she said, sitting down and twirling her sunglasses in her hand. "No, the decision to either drive slower or get a vehicle that would provide more protection in case of an accident."

"Mom, I can't begin to tell you how disturbing that comment is," I said.

"I'm sure you could, darling. But don't. I only stopped by to ask you why you aren't returning any of Jerry's phone calls."

I glared at her only because he wasn't around to bear the brunt of my anger. He'd called four times since yesterday's fiasco at breakfast. Each time I'd deleted the call without even bothering to listen to his messages. Now the big baby was again going behind my back and running to my mother. He'd struck out yesterday morning. Now he'd come to the plate again. Strike one, Jerry.

"Mom, I have no desire to speak with him. And I say this with all of the love and respect I can muster, but it's none of your business."

"Don't be ridiculous, darling," she said, smiling up at me. "Of course it is."

"Mom…" The combination of tone and my facial expression was the best warning shot I had in my arsenal.

"Look, darling, he's about to leave town, and I think he'd just like the chance to say goodbye. That's all."

"So he and his girlfriend have decided to ride off into the sunset together?"

"No," my mother said, shaking her head. "In fact, what he said was to tell you that Rosaline had changed her mind and he didn't have a clue where she was going to go. Does that make any sense to you?"

175

"Maybe a little," I said, glancing out over the River. "Has he finished whatever he was working on for you?"

"Yes," she said. "I have it in the car. Would you like to see it?"

"Absolutely not," I said, my voice quivering.

I was unable to maintain eye contact with her. Even though I often jokingly threatened to kill her for some of her actions done purportedly on my behalf, I couldn't bear the thought of reading a document that would force me to confront the reality that someday in the future she would be gone.

"Okay, darling," she whispered as she stood and embraced me.

A truck with a muffler fighting a bad cold pulled into the parking area. We watched Carl the Gardener hop out, closely followed by the Doberman that had threatened to eat us the night we'd snooped around his house. The dog bounded up onto the porch and sat down in front of me. I assumed he hadn't forgotten about the cookies. I reached into my pocket, let him take the cookie from my hand, and stroked its head.

"He's magnificent," my mother said.

"Yeah, he's a good-looking dog," I said, scratching the Doberman's ears.

"Who's talking about the dog, darling?"

I shook my head as I watched my mother prepare for Carl's arrival at the top of the steps.

"I think he falls outside your age formula, Mom."

"It's more of a guideline than a rule," she said.

The formula was one my mother's dating screening tools. This one dealt with the low end of the age range eligible for dating. Half her age plus seven was the general rule. Or as she just clarified; her guideline.

"Hi, Suzy," Carl said, glancing at me, then at the strange overt look my mother was giving him. "Hi, I'm Carl. You're the famous, Mrs. C, right?"

176

"I am indeed. And I'm delighted to meet you, Carl," she said, grasping his extended hand with both of hers.

Carl forced a smile and managed to free his without drawing too much attention to the effort. He stuffed both hands in the back pockets of his jeans for safe keeping.

"I don't have a reservation, but I was wondering if I could board Max overnight. I have to leave town for the day."

"I'm sure we can find room for him," I said. "Are you going to visit Chef Claire?"

"Yeah," he said. "Jackson made a call to the prison and vouched for me. They're going to let me see her this afternoon and maybe again for an hour tonight. I could probably make it back by midnight, but I don't like leaving Max in that situation for too long. Besides, I could use a chance of scenery. Maybe it'll help me get a good night's sleep."

Since I didn't have a clue what he was referring to, I merely nodded my head sympathetically.

"I gotta get on the road," he said, handing me Max's leash. "I'll swing by in the morning to pick him up."

"Not a problem, Carl," I said, attaching the leash to the dog's collar. "We'll take good care of him."

"Thanks," he said, then glanced at my mother. "It was nice meeting you, ma'am."

I choked back my laughter as we watched him drive off. My mother's mood turned dark. She glared after the truck, then caught the look on my face.

"Don't you dare say a word," she said, fishing in her shorts for her car keys.

"I wouldn't think of it...ma'am."

"Now, if you'll excuse me, I have a tee time with a delightful gentleman who appreciates a *mature* woman of substance."

"See you, Mom," I said, laughing. "Drive safe."

She waved over her shoulder, hopped into the SUV, and roared down the driveway.

I led Max inside and turned him over to Sammy. I found Josie in one of the exam rooms giving shots to a Golden Retriever puppy named Gabby.

"Have you ever seen anything this cute?" Josie said, beaming at the puppy.

"If I have, I don't remember," I said, stroking the dog's fur. "Guess who was just here?"

"Your mother," she said.

"Yeah, but that's not who I was talking about. Carl the Gardener."

"Really?" Josie said as she gently lifted the puppy into her arms. I followed her out into the reception area where a young girl and her mother sat waiting. Josie handed the puppy to the young girl. "She's perfect. And if you follow all the instructions I wrote down for you, she'll stay that way. Okay?"

"Got it," the girl said beaming as she cradled the puppy. "Thanks, Josie."

We waved goodbye as they made their way to checkout. Josie checked her schedule on her phone. "Good. I get a bit of a break. What a morning. So what did Carl want?"

"He dropped his dog off for boarding."

"Max? That gigantic Doberman who almost ate us that night?"

"Yeah."

"Let me guess, Carl is paying a visit to Chef Claire."

"He certainly is. You know what that means don't you?"

"Oh, I hope I don't," she said, frowning at me.

178

"His house is going to be empty all night."

"And you want to go out there and have a look?"

"Of course. Don't you?"

"Suzy, I want to do that about as much I want to be arrested for breaking and entering."

"Relax," I said, waving that prospect off. "We'll just take a quick look. We won't even touch anything."

"And what exactly do you expect to find?"

"I don't know," I said. "Maybe a clue. Or evidence. Like the murder weapon."

Josie shook her head and got up out of her chair.

"You're getting a little crazy with this one, Suzy," she said. "First of all, if you're right about a second knife, and I think you might be, by now, that knife is somewhere at the bottom of the River. And second, since when did Carl move back onto your list of prime suspects?"

"I'm not saying he did it," I said. "But I'm not convinced he didn't do it. Look, we know that he had been sleeping with Mrs. Crawford, right?"

"He's been sleeping with all of them," Josie said.

"Yeah, sure, I know that. But if Marge had promised him something, like giving him Candyland Island, and then changed her mind, that might have been enough to set him off in a rage."

"Carl? In a rage?" she said, laughing. "Suzy, he's a total stoner who constantly reeks of weed."

"Okay," I said, trying to regroup. "Then maybe he's protecting the killer."

"There you go again," she said. "Who is Carl protecting this time?"

"It must be Roxanne," I said, vigorously nodding my head.

179

"Suzy, we've been through this a dozen times," Josie said. "There is absolutely no evidence that connects her to anything other than an especially close relationship with the gardener."

"Exactly. And that's why we need to go out there tonight and take a look."

"Let me ask you this. If Carl is trying to cover up for Roxanne, why the heck would he even bother visiting Chef Claire? Wouldn't he just want her locked up and the case closed?"

"Maybe he's feeling guilty," I said. "He's conflicted. Or it's a smokescreen to keep the attention off him."

"You're unbelievable. I can't talk you out of this, can I?"

"You know better than that."

Josie sighed. "Okay, we'll go out there. But not until after dinner. I have a feeling we're both going to need all the strength we can get tonight."

"That's great. You're the best," I said, gently punching her arm. "And that reminds me. It's my turn to go grocery shopping. Anything you want me to pick up?"

"As a matter of fact," she said, digging through the pocket in her coat. "I have a list somewhere."

She pulled out a piece of paper and handed it to me. I unfolded the page and stared at the list that was long and extensive.

"That's a long list," I said.

"We're running low on some stuff, and I have a variety of cravings coming at me from several directions.

"This will take forever," I said as I continued examining the list.

"Consider it your penance for dragging me out in the middle of the night on another of your hair-brained schemes," she said, waving and laughing as she headed off to her next appointment.

I stuffed the list into my pocket and headed outside. I made the short drive to the Clay Bay Super Saver, the name a total misnomer since the owner was notorious for his outrageous prices, especially during the summer when he had a captive bunch of campers and tourists visiting the area. I found a parking spot right in front of the entrance, grabbed the biggest shopping cart I could, and went inside the busy store.

My progress was slowed by several conversations I had with various friends and Inn customers. The topic at the top of everyone's list was Marge Crawford's murder and the certain fate of Chef Claire. I kept my comments on the subject to a minimum and tried to redirect the conversation whenever possible. An hour later the shopping cart was overflowing, and I was down to a few items in the condiments aisle. I always saved these for last because they were a total pain to locate.

And Mr. Frank, the owner, had a very broad definition of what constituted a condiment. I finally located the brand of balsamic vinegar Josie wanted. And the kind of imported olives she liked. A couple of bottles of obscure hot sauces she'd discovered on a trip to Morocco that Mr. Frank special ordered just for her. A large jar of the dreaded Korean Kimchi which, to me, smelled like sweat socks left in a gym locker all summer.

I checked my list and scanned the overflowing cart. It was a bizarre collection of items, and if I weren't familiar with Josie's personal life, I would have sworn she was pregnant. I reached the maple syrup section and started to reach for a bottle of our usual choice, then stopped. I left the cart in the aisle and walked to the back of the store where I found Mr. Frank comparing a handful of order slips with a stack of recently delivered boxes. He'd owned the store since I was a kid and we'd been friends for a very long time. Now in his late seventies, he was moving a bit slower, but his mind was as sharp as ever. He glanced up when he saw me standing in the doorway and smiled.

"Suzy, it's so good to see you," he said, shuffling his way toward me and giving me a warm hug. "I always love it when you visit the store."

"That's because every time I come here, you're able to buy a new car," I said, laughing.

"What can I say?" he said. "You have expensive tastes. At least when it comes to food. How's your mom?"

"The usual," I said, shrugging. "Active and involved. Sticking her nose where it doesn't belong. You know, a total pain."

He laughed and shuffled to his desk and sat down.

"You got a bum knee, Mr. Frank?"

"More like a bum body," he said, shifting in his seat to get comfortable. "Word to the wise, Suzy. Never grow old."

"It still beats the alternative, right?"

"Yes, on most days," he said, winking at me. "Is there something you need help with?"

"Actually, yes, there is. I'm looking for a particular brand of maple syrup."

"Okay, which one?"

"Sugarland Farms," I said.

"Oh, my. Sugarland Farms," he said. "Now there's a blast from the past. I haven't heard that name in years."

"Did they go out of business?" I said.

"Let me think," he said, squinting as he tried to jog his memory. "I remember that it was a very popular brand and then it seemed to vanish off the shelves. I suppose they could have gone out of business, but my guess is that they got bought up by some conglomerate, and then the name got changed."

"Sure. That makes sense. Was it good?"

182

"Yes, if I remember correctly it was very good. But how many bad maple syrups have you ever had, Suzy?"

I laughed.

"None."

"There you go. I'm sorry I can't help you. But we've got quite a good selection of other brands."

"Yes," I said. "I'm familiar with all of them. Would you happen to remember where Sugarland Farms was based?"

"I wouldn't have a clue," he said, shaking his head. "But I imagine they were located fairly close to here. Back in those days, the distribution systems tended to be more regional. I'd say possibly Vermont, but my guess is that they were in Ontario or maybe somewhere in Quebec. Why do you want to know?"

"I had breakfast at the Café, and Eunice was telling me how good their maple syrup was, so I thought I'd give it a try."

"Eunice has a long memory," he said, laughing. Then he turned serious. "It's quite a nasty situation with Chef Claire."

"You know her?" I said.

"Of course," he said. "She handled all the ordering and shopping on the island. And since she was working for Bob Crawford, there were a lot of specialty items we needed to order. We got to know each other quite well over the past few months. She's even been over to our house for dinner a few times. Shirley is outraged that Jackson had the audacity to arrest her."

"It looks like they have some pretty incriminating evidence," I said.

"I don't care what they think they have," he snapped. "And I know Jackson is only doing his job, but that young woman didn't kill anybody."

"No, I agree. She didn't," I said, nodding. "Try not to be too hard on Jackson. He's in a tough spot."

183

"I suppose," he said, getting up out of his chair and grabbing the stack of order slips before shuffling over to the boxes that were piled high on the adjacent loading dock. "But he should know better. He can be such a little priss when it comes to following the rules." He winked at me and waved goodbye. "Just so we're clear, he gets that from his mother."

Sorry about that. I knew there was something I forgot to tell you.

Chapter 28

"This has to be the stupidest thing I've ever let you talk me into."

"I don't know, Josie," I said, hunched down behind a bush and peering at the house through my binoculars. "That's a pretty long list of choices."

"Well, this one has rocketed to the top of the charts," Josie said, swatting at a mosquito, then another. "I'm getting eaten alive out here. Where's that bug spray?"

"It's in my backpack," I said, continuing to peer at the house. Carl had left several lights on, but I didn't see any movement inside.

I wobbled in my crouched position as Josie noisily rummaged through the backpack I was wearing.

"You want some more?" Josie said.

"No, a gallon is my limit," I said. I lowered the binoculars and stood and stretched. I grimaced at the pain in my knees and lower back. "This detective work is a young woman's game."

"Detective work? I'd call it a Class 3 Misdemeanor. And that's before we've even gone inside."

"I thought you said that if I got you an ice cream cone before we came out here, you'd stop whining," I said.

"Obviously I lied," she said. "Okay, Sherlock, how do you want to play it?"

"I think the best way is just to walk up and knock on the door. And when nobody answers, we'll figure out the easiest way to get in and have a look around."

"And if somebody just happens to show up while we're in there, how do we explain ourselves?"

185

"We went over that in the car," I said, slapping at a mosquito. "Weren't you listening?"

"I was focused on my ice cream," she said. "You were pretty clear about my not getting any on your seats."

"Nice job with that, by the way," I said, making a mental note to schedule an appointment to have my car detailed.

"I should stick with two scoops," Josie said. "That third one is always tricky to keep on the cone."

"Yeah, so I noticed. Look, as I said in *the car*, if anybody does happen to show up, we'll explain ourselves by saying we thought we heard someone in distress inside the house. And it is highly unlikely that anyone will show up unannounced."

"You're probably right," Josie conceded. "The house is remote, and the chain across the driveway sends a pretty strong message."

"He obviously doesn't want uninvited guests popping in. It's not surprising since he's growing enough weed in his greenhouse to cure Glaucoma on both sides of the River."

"Did that just pop into your head or have you been working on that line all day?"

"It just popped in," I said, grinning in the dark. "It's a good one, huh?"

"Yeah, it's great," Josie said, flatly. "What if they don't believe us?"

"It's our word against theirs."

"Great plan, Suzy," Josie said.

Even though it was dark, I knew she was shaking her head at me.

"And if somebody does answer the door?" Josie said.

"We just tell them that we're looking for Carl and want to discuss the possibility of him handling the gardening at the Inn. It's perfect."

"Apart from the fact that we're showing up at his house in the middle of the night wearing backpacks and carrying binoculars."

186

"That's a good point," I said, sliding my backpack off and putting the binoculars inside. "Let's leave them here, and we'll pick them up on our way out. Good catch."

"No problem," Josie said. "It's the least I can do."

"You need to start thinking of this as an essential component of this case," I snapped. It didn't happen often, but sometimes Josie really made me cranky.

"Whatever. Let's just get this over with," Josie said, tossing her backpack on the ground next to mine.

We strolled up the gravel driveway until we reached the front steps. I stopped and glanced at Josie.

"You ready?" I said.

"Lead the way, Columbo."

I knocked on the front door and waited. Then I knocked a second time harder. The only sound we heard was the squeak the front door made as it partially opened.

"That's odd," I said, pushing my head through the opening. "Hello! Is anybody here?" I waited, then looked at Josie and shrugged. "Let's check it out."

I pushed the door all the way open and stepped into the living room bathed in light.

Josie followed me into the house, and we looked around the room. It was small but clean and nicely furnished. I glanced over my shoulder when Josie nudged me with her hand.

"What?"

Josie pointed at the far end of the living room that led to a hallway.

"Is that what I think it is?" Josie said.

"It looks like drops of blood," I said, starting to walk toward it.

She grabbed my arm and halted my progress.

187

"What do you think you're doing? I don't like this. We need to get out of here now," Josie said.

"No way," I said, resuming my walk across the room. "Suppose they need our help."

"So we call for help," Josie said. "My phone's right outside in my backpack."

"C'mon, Josie," I said. "We might not have time for that right now."

"You're such a piece of work," Josie said, shaking her head, but following me down the hallway.

The amount of blood continued to increase the further we went. It continued under the gap of a closed door, and I glanced back at Josie when I grasped the door handle.

"Are you ready for this?" I said, turning the handle.

"I guess there's no turning back now," she said.

I pushed the door open and gasped at what I saw.

"Oh, no," Josie said, gagging.

"Are you okay?" I said, glancing back and forth between her and the body on the tile floor.

"Well, I'm certainly doing better than her," Josie said, staring down at the body. "What on earth is going on in this town?"

"Go get our phones," I said. "I'll stay here to see if I can find a pulse."

"Good luck with that," Josie said, taking a quick glance at the body before running down the hall and out of the house.

I stared down at Roxanne's sprawled body and the gardening shears sticking out of her back. She was wearing what used to be a white bathrobe. I couldn't tell if she had just finished taking a shower or had been headed that way when she'd been attacked. I stretched out as far as I could without stepping in the blood and touched the side of her neck to check for a pulse. I couldn't detect anything.

188

Josie returned and handed me my phone. My hands shook as I dialed the number. I put the phone on speaker and tried to get some degree of control over my emotions.

"Hello, this is Jackson."

"Hi, Jackson."

"Suzy, what's up? Shouldn't you be in bed by now?"

"Without a doubt, Jackson. Look, you're not going to believe this, but... there's another situation that's come up."

"What have you done now, Suzy?"

"I haven't done anything," I said, staring down at the body. "But you and Freddie need to get out here."

"And where exactly might that be?"

"You remember Carl, the gardener for the Crawfords?"

"Sure," Jackson said, then paused. "Don't tell me he's dead?"

"No, but we're at his house," I said.

"We? Josie, you're there too aren't you?"

"Hi, Jackson," Josie said.

"You guys need to start focusing more on your dogs," Jackson said.

"Yeah, you're probably right," I said. "Do you know where Carl's house is?"

"The place off Route 12 with the chain across the driveway, right?"

"That's the one," I said. "It's locked, so you and Freddie will need to park on the side of the road and walk in. You'll see my car."

"Are you in any danger at the moment?"

"No, I think whoever did this is long gone," I said, glancing at Josie who nodded in agreement.

"Okay, we'll be right over," Jackson said. "By the way, who's the victim?"

"Roxanne."

189

"Crawford's girlfriend?"

"Yeah," I said.

"Lots of blood?"

"Yeah," I said.

"Maple syrup?"

"Not a drop in sight," I said.

"You know what to do, right?"

"Yes. Stay put and don't touch anything," I said.

"And that includes the fridge, too," Jackson said, then ended the call.

Chapter 29

"We need to stop meeting like this," Freddie deadpanned when I opened the front door.

Josie and I stepped back to give him and Jackson room to come inside. We didn't laugh at his joke, but it did break a bit of the tension we'd been dealing with the past half hour. Discovering a dead body in a strange house in the middle of the night is a bizarre and frightening experience.

I don't recommend it.

"Where is she?" Jackson said as he glanced around the living room.

"The bathroom at the end of the hall," I said, pointing briefly before sitting back down on the couch.

Both men headed off and moments later we heard the sound of gagging and coughing coming from the bathroom.

"I told you that you didn't have to feel bad about tossing your cookies," I said to Josie, who was still recovering from her initial reaction to seeing Roxanne sprawled on the bathroom floor.

"Suzy, I'm getting worried," she said.

"About what?"

"That we might be next," Josie said.

"No way," I said, shaking my head. "Why would anybody want to kill us?"

"For starters, because we keep sticking our noses where they don't belong."

"You worry too much," I said, trying not to think about the possibility that we could be targets.

"Yeah, that's the problem here," Josie said. "My worrying."

Jackson slowly wandered down the hall and sat down in a chair across from us. He removed his hat and wiped his face and neck with a handkerchief. He stared at us, seemingly unsure of where to start.

"What a mess," Jackson said. "I should have taken my dad's advice and just learned the grocery business."

"You'd be bored in a week," I said.

"At the moment, boredom sounds pretty good," he said. "Okay, let's get started. What on earth were you two doing here in the first place?"

I glanced at Josie, who shook her head as she stared off into the distance. Apparently, I was on my own.

"Well, Josie and I have been thinking about having some landscape work done so we thought we'd swing by and ask Carl if he might be interested in the job."

Jackson gave me a blank, almost hostile, stare.

"Try again," he said, sitting back in his chair.

I exhaled, then nodded.

"Okay, Carl brought his dog in to be boarded today since he was going to visit Chef Claire."

"Yes, I know. I made a call to the prison," Jackson said.

"So he said. That was such a nice thing to do, Jackson."

"Drop the empathy act, Suzy," he said. "I'm not in the mood."

"Sorry. Anyway, after Carl left, we thought that-"

"Excuse me?" Josie said, glaring at me.

"What?"

"You're doing the collective *we* thing again," Josie said.

Okay, I was flying solo on this one.

"After he left, *I* thought it would be a good idea to come out and have a look around."

"So you were snooping," Jackson said.

192

"Snooping is such a harsh term," I said, then nodded. "Yeah, okay, we were snooping."

"But I was doing it under protest," Josie said.

"Save it, Josie," Jackson said. "I'll get to you as soon as I finish with Ms. Meddler here."

Before I could turn indignant and fight back, Freddie came racing down the hall holding his phone against his ear.

"Yes, that's the address," Freddie said, frantically talking into the phone. "Get that ambulance out here now! You'll see a chain across the driveway but just blow right through it. And bring several pints of type O blood. Do it now!"

Freddie put his phone away and looked at Jackson.

"I found a trace of a pulse. Just strong enough to tell me she's still alive," he said, heading back toward the bathroom.

Jackson raced after him. Stunned by the news, Josie and I sat quietly on the couch. I felt the tears well up in my eyes and then they began streaming down my face. Josie took one look at me and lost it as well. We were still bawling our eyes out when the ambulance arrived a few minutes later.

We sat unmoving on the couch for the next two hours as paramedics, and a local doctor arrived and performed their magic on Roxanne in the bathroom. Jackson joined us in the living room, and we listened to his side of the conversation as he made several calls. We learned that an all-points bulletin had been put out to locate Carl. He also called the prison where Chef Claire was to have the staff interview her regarding what she and Carl had discussed during his visit. He spoke with the state policeman we'd met the day Marge Crawford was killed. Twenty minutes later he arrived at the house, and Jackson briefed him on the situation before escorting him to the bathroom where the medical staff continued to work frantically to save Roxanne's life.

193

"He's really good at his job," I said to Josie after Jackson had headed down the hall.

"Yes, he is," Josie said. "I'm sorry I snapped at you earlier."

"Don't worry about it, I said, patting her hand. "I deserved it."

"Yes, you certainly did," she said managing a small laugh.

"Who do you think did this?" I said.

"I have no idea," she said. "But those gardening shears were embedded right up to the handle. Whoever did this would have to be really strong."

"You mean strong like Carl?"

"Yeah, strong like Carl," Josie said.

"I guess I can see that," I said, my mind refusing to shut down. "Carl goes out of town with a perfect alibi, rents a motel room, drives home after he talks with Chef Claire, takes care of Roxanne, then heads back to the motel. It's a lot of driving, but the timeframe works."

"Suzy?" Josie said.

"Yeah."

"If you don't stop talking, I swear I'm going to punch you," Josie said.

"No, just listen to what I'm- Ow! That hurt," I said, grabbing my shoulder.

"I said stop talking."

Josie glared at me, and I finally got the message.

"That's gonna leave a mark," I said, rubbing the tender spot.

"Good."

Freddie appeared in the hall and watched as two paramedics wheeled a stretcher past him and out the door. Roxanne was strapped tight and connected to oxygen and a blood bag. We watched until the ambulance, siren blaring, roared down the gravel driveway and disappeared. Freddie, sweating profusely, sat in a chair and stared down at the floor.

"Is she going to make it?" I whispered.

194

Freddie looked up and seemed startled to see us there. He nodded and wiped his forehead with the back of his hand.

"Yeah, I think she has a chance," he said. "I have no idea how she managed to hang on. I've never seen anything like it. The garden shears missed her heart by half an inch, but given the amount of blood she lost she should be dead."

Jackson and state policeman walked into the living room and remained standing.

"We're going to need to speak with both of you," Jackson said.

Josie and I nodded.

"She was very lucky you guys were here," Freddie said, continuing to come out of his daze. "In a weird way, you might have saved her life."

I probably should have felt somewhat better when I heard him say that, but for some reason, Josie and I started bawling again. To their credit Jackson and the state policeman waited out the next fifteen minutes in silence until we stopped.

Chapter 30

Getting my day off the ground reminded me of what it's like when you're trying to start your car on a frigid winter morning. The car wants to start; it probably wants to get warm even more than you do. After all, it was the one sitting outside all night while you were sleeping in a warm bed. But despite its best efforts to get going, it struggles as all the moving parts try to find a way to work together and get all the cylinders firing at the same time.

It was almost four in the morning when Jackson and state policeman finished with us. After an hour of questioning, it became clear that Josie and I weren't suspects. But they kept asking their questions, many of them repeated, hoping our answers would provide some clues or insights into what was going on in and around our beloved town.

I refilled my coffee mug and sat down at my desk and fired up my laptop. As soon as she was sure my movements didn't involve food, Chloe hopped up on the couch and propped her head on her outstretched paws and kept a close eye on things. My phone rang, and I checked the number.

"Good morning, Jackson," I said, yawning. "You're up early."

"I haven't been to bed," he said. "I thought I'd just check in to see how you and Josie are doing."

"We're fine," I said. "And I'm sorry about all the sobbing and emotional outbursts. Sometimes I can be such a girl."

Jackson laughed. I could hear the fatigue in his voice.

"Thanks for clarifying that," he said. "Don't worry about it. And don't tell anybody, but I was on the verge of tears a couple of times myself."

"Did you track Carl down?" I took a sip of coffee and carried it to the couch. I sat down and waited for Chloe to climb aboard and make herself comfortable.

"Yeah, the state police out of Rochester found him sound asleep in the motel. And they brought him back just before sunrise."

"And?"

"And he's probably sound asleep at his house," Jackson said. "That is if he's able to sleep there given what went down last night."

"So you didn't arrest him?" I said.

"No, his alibi checked out completely. He was at the prison last night visiting with Chef Claire until around eight. Then he ate dinner at a restaurant near his motel. And the motel clerk confirmed that Carl picked up his room key just before ten."

"That's good. I was hoping he didn't do it," I said. "But what about the greenhouse?"

"What about it?" Jackson said.

"Didn't you check it out?"

"Of course we checked it out," he said.

"And?"

"What is this, Suzy? Twenty questions? And what?"

"Didn't you find something in the greenhouse?"

"Suzy, I have no idea what you're talking about. But I don't think I can arrest a guy just for thinking he could grow hothouse orchids in a cold climate like this." Then Jackson laughed. "I suppose I could hold him for psychiatric observation. I mean, who would be crazy enough to come up with that idea?"

"He's growing orchids?"

"Yeah. And he's doing a good job of it, too. I wouldn't have thought it was possible. What did you think he was growing in there?"

197

"Uh, well, I was thinking he might be growing something of a more *herbal* variety."

"Weed? If he's growing weed, he sure isn't growing it in his greenhouse."

"How about that," I said, glancing up at Josie entered the office.

"Anyway, he was shocked to hear about what happened to Roxanne. He's blaming himself for not being there to protect her."

"Good morning, Jackson," Josie said.

"Hey, Josie. How are you doing?"

"I'm exhausted," she said. "I'm walking around in a total fog this morning. I don't know how you do your job."

"Yeah, I've been wondering the same thing myself lately."

"How's Roxanne doing?" I said.

"She's still in critical condition at Upstate Medical. But the doctors are *cautiously optimistic*. Their words, not mine. That's one tough woman."

Josie and I both nodded.

"I'm glad to hear you two are okay," Jackson said. "That was a lot to deal with. Look, I need to head off. I'm going back out to Carl's place for another walkthrough with the forensic folks. I'll check in with you later."

He ended the call, and Josie arched her back and yawned. Then she noticed my laptop.

"What are you doing?"

"I decided to take your advice about dealing more in fact than just my emotions and gut instincts," I said, tapping my laptop with one hand. "I'm doing a bit of research on Sugarland Farms. I'm curious about why a popular brand that people still remember just disappeared."

"Good for you. A little internet research should keep you out of trouble," Josie said as she started opening and closing various drawers and

198

cupboards and coming up empty. Then she stopped and looked at me with a confused expression. "What's Sugarland Farms?"

"It's the maple syrup company that Eunice mentioned at breakfast the other day. Both she and Jackson's dad said that their syrup was great, but the company seems to have completely disappeared from history. Since maple syrup was part of both Crawford's crime scenes, I thought I'd check it out. We're a little short on clues at the moment."

"Take all the time you need on the computer. I could use a quiet day," she said, laughing. Then she resumed looking for whatever she'd lost.

"Yeah, I suppose I could use a day out of the doghouse," I said, tapping the keyboard. "But I've been Googling all morning and can't find anything except a couple of obscure references that don't make any sense to me."

"Well, a lot of things that happened before the internet haven't made their way online yet. And I imagine some never will. The history of this Sugarland Farms is probably locked away in the musty archives of some small town newspaper or public library."

"Probably," I said, looking up from the screen at the sound of drawers opening and closing. "What on earth are you looking for?"

"My bacon and egg breakfast bagel," Josie said, opening the drawer where we kept office supplies.

"And you think it's in there with the paper clips and staples?"

"I have no idea where I put it," Josie said, pausing from her search. "I was in here earlier looking for a box of manila folders. I had it on a plate, and I remember setting it down." She snapped her fingers. "Now I remember." She used a footstool to climb up on the counter and reached for the top of the cabinet. "Aha," she exclaimed, grabbing the edge of the plate. Then she climbed down and stared at the empty plate in her hands. "That's odd." Then she gave Chloe a look of mock indignation.

"You ate my bagel? How could you?"

199

Chloe cocked her head and looked away; not guilt-ridden by any stretch of the imagination, but without a doubt caught red-handed after the fact.

"How the heck did you get all the way up there?" Josie said, sitting down on the couch and rubbing Chloe's head. "You're worse than a toddler."

The office door opened, and my mother's head appeared.

"Speaking of things worse than a toddler," I said.

"Am I interrupting?" she said, walking inside.

"Constantly," I said. "What's going on, Mom?"

"Oh, I thought I'd just stop by and congratulate my two heroes," she said, beaming with pride. "The town is simply buzzing about how you saved that poor woman's life last night."

"Mom, the people who saved Roxanne's life were the medical people. Josie and I were just lucky to show up when we did."

"Don't be modest, darling," she said, sitting down on the couch next to Chloe.

I was shocked because my mother normally kept her distance from all four-legged creatures. Chloe hopped onto her lap, and my mother began to gently stroke her fur. Josie watched for a moment, then gave me the '*What the heck is happening*' look. I shrugged and looked back at the couch where Chloe had flipped over expecting a tummy rub. My mother complied, and I watched her meticulously groomed and painted nails start to trail up and down the dog's stomach. Chloe kicked a leg, and her tongue hung from the corner of her mouth.

"You like that, don't you?" my mother said, laughing. "What a good girl. Who's the good girl?"

"Mom?" I said with genuine concern. "Are you okay? Did you fall and hit your head or something?"

"No, darling," she said, continuing to put Chloe in a trance. "I'm fine."

200

"Okay," I said, again glancing briefly at Josie. "If you say so." Then the lightbulb went on. "Wait a minute," I said, staring at her. "Who is he?"

"What on earth are you talking about, darling?" she said, flashing me a coy smile.

"Your newfound love for dogs," I said. "Let me guess. Your new flame is a dog lover. No, that wouldn't be enough by itself. Wait a minute, you're dating a vet, aren't you?"

My mother smiled at me and nodded.

"Very good, darling. You got it in on your first try."

Josie roared with laughter.

"Ah, Mrs. C., you are too much," Josie said. "Who is it?"

"If you must know, he's a lovely widower in his late forties with a very successful veterinary practice outside of Syracuse," she said, increasing the speed of her tummy rub which caused both of Chloe's legs to kick uncontrollably. My mother watched the dog's reaction, and her eyes danced.

"Jim Wilkins?" Josie said.

"Yes, it is," my mother said. Surprised, she looked up at Josie. "How do you know Jim?"

"We run into each other at various meetings and the occasional conference. He's a great guy. Well done, Mrs. C."

"Thanks, dear. Yes, he is wonderful."

"Absolutely," Josie said. "All the female vets, including me, think he's very sexy."

"Please don't tell me you're interested in him, Josie. If you are, I'll just fold my tent right now."

I laughed as my mother spread her hands and looked at me.

"I mean, just look at her," my mother said, shrugging to emphasize her point. "How does anyone compete with that?"

201

"Interested in Jim? Not a chance," Josie said, shaking her head. "He's way too old for me."

"Well, fortunately, his age is not a problem for me," she said, resuming Chloe's tummy rub.

"Yeah, you got lucky, Mom. He's around fifty, and since your dating formula is half your age plus seven, it looks like he just made it in under the wire."

"That is not funny, darling," she said, then nodded at my laptop. "What on earth are you doing?"

"I'm trying to find out anything I can about an old maple syrup company. Sugarland Farms."

"Sugarland Farms," she said, nodding. "I remember them."

"Really?" I said.

"Sure. It was a very popular brand when I was younger. Now that I think about, they just disappeared." She gently slid out from underneath Chloe to stand and brush herself off. "I need to run."

"Do you remember anything about the company?" I said.

"Not really. Other than the fact that they made great syrup. But if it's that important you could always head up to Smithville and check it out. I'm sure there are still some people around who remember it."

"Smithville?"

"Yeah," my mother said. "It's a small town about half an hour outside of Ottawa. It's only about an hour and a half from here at the most."

"They were based out of Smithville?"

"Yes," she said. "I remember because the town was always mentioned in their commercials. Something about how their syrup was sweeter than a Smithville sunset. It was one of those annoying jingles you couldn't get out of your head."

202

She gave Chloe one final ear scratch, then waved goodbye and strolled out of the office. I looked at Josie who was frowning and staring at the wall. She knew what was coming.

"Do I even need to ask?" I said.

"No, I'll go clear my afternoon," she said, getting up out of her chair. "And then we're done with this thing, right?"

"Oh, without a doubt."

Judging from the look on her face as she left, I'm not quite sure she believed me.

Chapter 31

As we always did whenever we drove across the Thousand Islands Bridge that led to Wellesley Island then ultimately the Canadian mainland, Josie and I fell silent as we neared the apex and looked around in both directions at the sight below. The sun was bright, the wind low, and the water below was a dark blue sheet of glass interspersed with islands of various sizes. Even though I'd seen it hundreds of times throughout my life, it still took my breath away.

At the Canadian Immigration checkpoint, the official played twenty questions with us, primarily because he wanted to prolong his time ogling Josie who was in the passenger seat. I'm sure his final question would have been to ask for her phone number, but the line of cars behind ours grew to the point when he was finally forced to wave us on our way with a sad smile.

"I think he was trying to come up with a reason to give you a cavity search," I said.

Josie laughed.

"Actually, I think he was checking you out," she said.

"Yeah, right," I said. "What's the road we take off of 15?"

Josie checked the map.

"Left on Route 43, stay on that for about five miles, then right on 511 and that will take us right into Smithville. Easy."

"You think we should have asked Jackson to come with us?" I said.

"No, probably not," she said, adjusting the passenger seat to a reclining position. "He's buried at the moment, and if this turns out to be a total waste of time, which I have a feeling it will, that would only give Jackson one more reason to get mad at us."

"I thought we'd stop at that bakery in Gananoque on the way back," I said.

"Oooh, Panache. What a great idea," she said. "You're offering just to make sure I don't get to use the *total waste of time* crack again, aren't you?"

"Yup. But we are running a bit low on sweets at the house."

"Yeah, sorry about that," Josie said. "I went overboard last night when we finally got home."

Overboard? She'd eaten enough desserts to put a kindergarten class into a sugar coma. No wonder she hadn't been able to get to sleep. But she was doing her best to catch up now as the car ride and comfortable leather seat worked their magic. She snored softly in the passenger seat, forcing me to turn the music up a bit.

An hour later I pulled into the small parking lot in front of the Smithville Gazette, a local weekly newspaper that *printed everything you needed to know*. At least that's what the faded wood sign on the front of the building said. But who was I to disagree? I nudged Josie awake and hopped out of the car and looked around. Josie climbed out and arched her back to stretch.

"It's Clay Bay without the water," she said.

"Yeah, that about sums it up," I agreed.

I pointed at the front door, and we walked inside. Either all the staff was out covering breaking news, or things were pretty quiet in Smithville. The space looked like it was converted from an old general store, or perhaps a small manufacturing operation of some sort. But it was immaculate, and its polished wood floors glistened in the sunlight that poured in through two massive picture windows on the far side of the building. A woman in her sixties came out of an office on one side and approached the front counter where we were standing.

"I thought I heard somebody come in," she said. "May I help you?"

We introduced ourselves, and she listened as I provided a quick overview of the reason behind our visit. I left out the part about how our snooping – I referred to it as research – was connected to the recent rash of murders in Clay Bay. She nodded and then opened the door that led past the counter into what she called the newsroom.

"How long has the Gazette been in business, Mrs. Johnson?"

"1897," she said, glancing around the room with pride. "I bought it twenty-three years ago. And despite the best efforts of the internet to kill off every bit of newsprint, we're hanging in there."

"I'm glad to hear that," I said.

That was true. I was. She seemed like a nice woman, and every town should have a local newspaper that provided a bit of common ground for the people who lived there.

"In the morning, there's just something special about holding your coffee in one hand and a newspaper in the other."

"I'm not familiar with that," Josie said.

"You're not a coffee drinker, dear?" Mrs. Johnson said.

"Oh, I drink it all the time," Josie said. "I just never have a free hand to hold the paper."

"What's in your other hand?"

"Usually, a sandwich," Josie said, laughing.

"Oh, you're an eater," she said, laughing along. "Me too. And it shows." She took a step back and gave Josie the once over. "You must exercise a lot."

"Well, I do spend a lot of time on wild goose chases," Josie said.

She is so going to pay for that crack.

"Sugarland Farms," Mrs. Johnson said as she opened a door that led downstairs. She turned the lights on. "I haven't heard that name in years."

"Do you remember the company?" I said, carefully making my way down the wooden stairs leading to a large basement.

"I remember the story," she said, pausing to look around and get her bearings among the shelves and boxes that filled most of the floor space. "But it happened before I moved here and bought the paper."

She headed for a stack of shelves along one of the walls and put her glasses on to read the labels.

"Here we go," she said. "I think it was around 1985, maybe 86." She removed her glasses and looked at us. "I should probably buy a scanner and get all this digitized, but somehow that seems sacrilegious. Does that make any sense?"

"Actually, it does," I said.

"Well, I'm going to leave you to it," she said. "I'll be here all day so take all the time you need. And if you have any questions, just let me know."

"Thanks so much, Mrs. Johnson," I said.

She waved and slowly made her way up the stairs.

"What was all that about digitization?" Josie said.

"She was saying that while you can't fight the advancement of technology, you don't have to turn over all your life history to it."

"Really?" Josie said, frowning. "Must be newspaper speak."

I chuckled and turned toward the shelf. Together, we lifted two boxes labeled 1985 and carefully placed them on a nearby table. Inside were copies of all fifty-two Smithville Gazette editions for that year. Each one was covered with a clear plastic bag that seemed to be doing a decent job preserving the newsprint. We went through them in order, starting with the first week in January. In a late August edition, we hit the first mention of Sugarland Farms.

"Here's a story about the pending sale of Sugarland," Josie said.

I leaned over her shoulder and read along.

207

"But it doesn't mention the buyer," I said.

"No," she said, scanning the rest of the article. She flipped through the rest of the paper, then closed it and slid it back into its plastic bag while I grabbed the next week's edition.

"Here's another story about it," I said. "It says the sale of Sugarland Farms while turning contentious is still on track." I read the rest of the article and frowned when I finished. "The reporter didn't dig very deep."

"It must have been a huge story in town," Josie said. "It doesn't seem like the sort of place where a lot of big news would be made."

"Neither's Clay Bay," I said, moving onto the next week's edition.

"Good point," Josie said. "But I'd expect to see a lot more details."

"Maybe somebody gave the reporter a bit of cash to go easy on the specifics," I said.

We found another mention of the sale being finalized in one of the December editions, then continued into 1986. In February, we hit the motherlode.

"Wow," I said, reading the headline. "Valentine's Day Murder-Suicide Rocks Smithville."

Josie leaned over my shoulder to read the article.

"Jonathan Wilson, former owner of Sugarland Farms. Geez, he shot his wife, then killed himself. And in front of their six-year-old daughter. Who could do that?"

"I have no idea. What could have possibly provoked him to do something like that?"

"I need to sit down," Josie said, looking away from the photos. "I feel sick to my stomach."

While she recovered, I kept reading. There was one more reference in a June edition.

208

"The daughter started exhibiting strange behaviors about four months after she saw it happen," I said.

"Can't blame her for that," Josie said. "What happened to her?"

"It sounds like she was either institutionalized or put in a foster home. I can't tell from the way this is written. But the article mentions frequent episodes of sub-psychotic rage."

We turned around when he heard the sound of footsteps coming down the stairs. Mrs. Johnson headed toward us carrying a small shoebox.

"I found this upstairs in one of our closets," she said. "We like to save old advertising and marketing trinkets from local companies when we come across them. It looks like there are a couple of Sugarland items in here. I thought you might like to see them."

"Thanks, Mrs. Johnson," I said.

She handed us the shoebox and headed back up the stairs. Josie started rummaging through the box.

"Here's an old contest they ran for schoolkids. All they had to do was send in three labels for a chance to win a tour of the Sugarland facility. And here are the words to their jingle. And your mom remembered correctly. Sweeter than a Smithville sunrise."

I glanced down at the words to the jingle that were written out in the manner they were supposed to be sung. It reminded me of the *follow the bouncing ball* sing-along technique that occasionally still showed up in commercials.

"It would help if we knew the tune to sing," I said.

Then a lightbulb went off.

I silently sang the words to the children's song still stuck in my head from the other day.

"Wow," I said.

"What is it?" Josie said.

209

"The girl was six when it happened, right?" I said.

"Yeah," Josie said.

"That would put her in her late-thirties now," I said heading for the stairs as various ideas and questions exploded in my head.

"Where are you going?" Josie said, climbing to her feet.

"To ask Mrs. Johnson where the local cemetery is," I said, bouncing up the stairs two at a time.

Like most places in Smithville, the cemetery wasn't far away. We covered the three miles in less than ten minutes, and that included making a wrong turn on one of the winding country roads that seemed to surround the town. I stopped the car next to a strand of trees that ran along the outer perimeter of the cemetery and turned it off. Another car was parked on the same side of the road about two hundred yards ahead of ours.

My chest heaved as I tried to both catch my breath and deal with the adrenaline rush flowing through my body. Josie stared at me like I'd lost my mind.

"Hand me my binoculars," I said.

Josie opened the glove box and handed them to me. I tore them from their case and took a look at the parked car. Then I scanned the cemetery. I stopped when I saw the back of a lone woman kneeling down in front of a headstone arranging several pots of plants and flowers.

"What on earth is going on?" Josie said, her face a mixture of concern and bewilderment.

"Take a look," I said, handing her the binoculars.

She held the binoculars up and stared at the woman kneeling in front of the grave.

"Is that Rosaline?" she said.

"Yes. It certainly is."

"She's the daughter? The six-year-old who watched her dad murder her mother and then kill himself?"

"It has to be her," I said.

"But what's the connection with the Crawfords?" Josie said, taking another look through the binoculars.

"My guess is that Crawford was the one who bought Sugarland Farms. I don't have a clue why it wasn't mentioned in the stories."

"But she works for his company," Josie said.

"Not only that, if it plays out the way she wants, she's going to be running it."

"So this whole thing was a set up to get control of the company?"

"I think that's part of it," I said, taking the binoculars back for another look. "But primarily Rosaline must be out for revenge."

"What do we do now?"

"Now that's a very good question," I said, lowering the binoculars with a frown on my face. "What do you want to do?"

"Well, I'm certainly not going to confront her. It's pretty clear that she still has issues."

Despite the seriousness and potential danger of our situation, I laughed at Josie's deadpan delivery.

"Yeah, issues like sub-psychotic rage," I said. "But we can't just let her drive off. The other day at breakfast she mentioned something about going into hiding. At the time I thought she was being overly dramatic with her *I'm in danger* routine."

"I'm sure her plan is to disappear," Josie said.

"But why come here first?"

It was such a good question, I thought I'd take a shot answering it.

"To say goodbye to her parents one more time?" I said. "Maybe to tell them that she's finally avenged their death?"

211

"Or maybe to spit on their graves," Josie said. "I don't want to spend too much time thinking about what's rolling around inside her head, Suzy."

"Yeah, I get that," I said, nodding. "We need to figure out a way to keep her here for a while."

"I have an idea," Josie said, searching inside her purse. "Just drive past her car and let me out. Then wait for me at the other end of the cemetery."

"What are you going to do?"

Josie held up a metal object that was inside a small plastic case. I recognized it immediately.

"You always carry a scalpel inside your purse?" I said, shaking my head in disbelief.

"You never know when it will come in handy," she said, smiling. "Like right now."

"And in your hands, it sure beats a can of pepper spray," I said, putting the car in gear.

"You got that right," she said.

I slowed the car as we approached Rosaline's vehicle and Josie hopped out and ducked down alongside the driver's side that was adjacent to the road. I continued down the road and then pulled to the side and stopped. I watched Josie use the scalpel to puncture all four tires and jog back to the car. I pulled out my phone and dialed Jackson's number.

"Jackson, it's me," I said when he answered.

Josie hopped into the passenger seat out of breath, and I continued down the road away from the cemetery.

"Hey, Suzy. Are you staying out of trouble?" Jackson said.

"Hey, Jackson," Josie managed to get out.

"Hi, Josie," he said, laughing. "Did some lucky guy get you breathing that hard or were you just thinking about me?"

"Funny, Jackson. You're a real hoot."

212

I explained to him where we were, what we'd done, and what we'd found out. He listened closely and then exhaled loudly through the phone.

"Wow," he said. "What a weird story. Look, I don't want you getting anywhere near Rosaline, but is it possible for you guys keep an eye on her until I can get the Canadian cops on the scene?"

"That won't be necessary, Jackson," I said. "She won't be going anywhere for a while." I glanced through the rearview mirror and watched as Rosaline kicked massive dents in her car upon discovering the four flat tires. "But make sure you tell the Canadians to be prepared for battle. She's in a pretty bad mood at the moment, and I don't see it improving."

"Got it," Jackson said. "Nice job. Now, why don't you do everyone a favor and head back home and play with your dogs?"

"We're going to do exactly that as soon as we make one more stop," I said, glancing at Josie.

"That's right. The bakery. I almost forgot."

I tossed my phone in my bag and sped down the road. I took one more look through the mirror at Rosaline who continued screaming and trying to kick and punch her car into oblivion.

"So that's what sub-psychotic rage looks like?" I said.

"Yup," Josie said, glancing over her shoulder to watch the out of control Rosaline disappear in the distance. "Textbook case."

"I guess that explains why she was able to throw Crawford overboard."

"Yeah," Josie said. "And Roxanne is a very lucky woman."

"That's for sure," I said, nodding as I turned onto a side road that led back to the highway. "I get why she'd go after the Crawfords. But why would Rosaline try to kill Roxanne?"

"I don't know, Suzy," Josie said, yawning. "Maybe just because she's nuts."

213

I fell silent and drifted off into deep thought as I drove through the light rain that had started falling. Josie sat up when she heard the sound of the windshield wipers and looked at me.

"You're wondering if Jerry the Lawyer is in this thing with her, aren't you?"

"Yup. That thought has crossed my mind," I said. "What's your take on it?"

"Suzy, I'd rather think about anything else but that at the moment if it's okay with you," Josie said, leaning back in her seat and closing her eyes.

"Yeah, that's a good idea. I guess it can wait," I said, focusing on the road. "You hungry?"

"I could eat."

Chapter 32

I watched Josie put the finishing touches on an elaborate bandage that covered the back left foot of a Lab that had skidded along a wooden dock while chasing a tennis ball and gotten a huge splinter jammed between the pads of its paw. The young woman who owned the Lab was nervously pacing in the exam room and wincing every time she heard her dog whimper. Josie had decided there was no need to use anesthesia on the dog, so it was up to Sammy and me to keep the dog calm and immobile. Sammy handled the lower half and legs while I stroked the Lab's head and whispered gently in its ear.

"There we go," Josie said, standing up and removing her latex gloves. She turned to the owner. "She'll be fine. It's a nasty cut, and she'll be limping around for a few days, but that's to be expected. If I got a six-inch splinter jammed between my toes, I'd be bawling like a baby. I gave her a sedative, so she'll be groggy for a while, but when she wakes up, you need to make sure she doesn't start chewing the bandage. If she does and you can't get her to stop, give me a call, and we'll talk about putting a neck collar on her. I hate them, but sometimes it's all you can do."

"Okay, Doc. Thanks so much."

"Sammy, would you mind carrying her out to Mindy's car and then following her home to help Maxine get settled in?"

"Sure," Sammy said, gently picking the dog up.

"And it's almost quitting time," Josie said. "Why don't you just call it a day after that?"

"Thanks," Sammy said on his way out the door. "I'll see you guys in the morning."

215

I waved goodbye and followed Josie through the exam room door that led to the back of the Inn. I looked around, and all the dogs were in their condos eating dinner. I did a quick check-in with Jill who was handling dinner hour, reviewed tomorrow's schedule, and finally ran out of things to do and headed up to the house.

I jumped in the shower, and by the time I made my way downstairs to the living room wearing sweats and a tee shirt, Josie was already there drinking wine and chatting with Jackson who was still in his uniform and drinking coffee. I was beginning to wonder if he was ever officially off the clock.

"Hey, Suzy," he said. "I thought I'd drop by and give you an update."

"And take the opportunity to try and wrangle a date?" I said, chuckling as I sprawled out on the couch.

"I'm still holding out hope that my dogged persistence will eventually win out over my apparent lack of sex appeal," Jackson said, laughing.

"Don't be too hard on yourself, Jackson," Josie said. "I'm sure there are lots of women who think you have tons of appeal."

"Just not you, right?"

Josie flashed him a quick smile and took a sip of wine.

"So what's the deal with Rosaline?" I said, sitting up on the couch and folding my legs underneath me.

"She's lawyered up and silent at the moment," Jackson said. "They put her in protective custody in a psych ward. Twenty-four hour armed guard lockdown."

"Has she owned up to anything?" I said.

"She finally admitted to being the daughter. But that's it," Jackson said.

"She's smart enough to know that she wouldn't be able to get away with that lie," I said.

216

"Yeah, you can't get around the DNA," Jackson said. "The Canadian cops said she was out of her mind with rage when they picked her up at the cemetery. It took three of them to get her into the police car."

"I guess the four flat tires did the trick," I said, shaking my head at the memory.

"Just call me the fastest scalpel in the West," Josie said, laughing.

"Did you ask her about the key?" I said.

"Yeah, I even showed it to her," Jackson said. "No reaction at all. She just looked at it and then stared off at the wall. But she was pretty out of it on all the medication they're giving her."

"There has to be some connection between the key and the murders," I said.

"There could be. But when it comes to the Crawfords and Roxanne, she isn't talking. And her alibis are solid. She was getting busy with her boyfriend when all three happened, and each one was confirmed by the motel manager where the boyfriend has been staying. He said their sessions went on for hours and that they made so much noise they embarrassed the other guests."

"See what you missed out on?" Josie deadpanned, then looked at Jackson and laughed.

"Shut up," I said, throwing one of the couch pillows at her. I looked at Jackson. "So what now?"

"I don't know," he said. "All I have is a woman with some serious mental problems caused by a traumatic childhood experience. The shrink who's seeing her says Rosaline exhibits serious cognitive dissonance punctuated with episodes of intermittent explosive disorder."

"That's the clinical term for she's off her rocker," Josie deadpanned.

"Thanks, but I got that one," I said.

Josie laughed and got up to refresh Jackson's coffee.

217

"So what now?" I said.

"Well," Jackson said, choosing his words carefully. "We thought we might try to put the squeeze on the boyfriend to see if we can shake anything loose that might poke a hole in their alibis."

I looked at Josie, and she shook her head. We both knew what was coming next.

"I guess that's worth a shot," I whispered.

"I was wondering if you might be willing to help out," he said.

"You want me to do the squeezing?" I said, glancing at Josie.

"If you're comfortable with the idea," Jackson said. "I know it sounds like it might be dangerous, but we'd do it in a public place and have a lot of people there undercover just in case things got ugly."

"He wouldn't hurt me," I said, shaking my head.

"How do you know that?" Jackson said.

"For one reason, he has a strong attraction for me I really can't explain. And second, he's not a killer. He might be an enabler, but not a killer."

"I'm not sure I like this idea, Suzy," Josie said. "Given the number of times you've been wrong on this thing, how can you be so sure?"

"I'll be fine," I said. "I'll invite him to dinner at Tondeuse."

"And we'll do our usual, right?" she said.

I looked at her and realized she wasn't joking. I thought about it, then nodded.

"Yes, I'll text you straight away if it looks like things are starting to head south."

"What are you two talking about?" Jackson said.

"It's a system we have for getting each other out of bad dates," Josie said. "We text each other if we want to get out of a date. And then the other just pops in unexpectedly and sits down at the table, thereby effectively ending the date."

218

"You really do that?" Jackson said, glancing back and forth at us.

"Sure. All the time," I said. "And if you were ever able to convince Josie to go out with you, I'm sure you'd get a chance to see it in action firsthand."

Josie roared with laughter. Jackson didn't find it quite as funny.

"Okay, let's set it up for tomorrow night," he said.

"All right," I said, shrugging.

"And Josie and I will be waiting at the bar for your text message," he said, beaming at her.

"We will?" Josie said.

"Yes, we will. And since this will be an official police operation, you have no choice but to accept."

Josie thought about it for a long time, then nodded in agreement.

"Congratulations, Jackson," she said, finishing her wine. "You finally figured out a way to finagle a dinner date out of me."

"Yeah, I did," he said through a huge grin. "How about that? And all I had to do was play my *your roommate might be in trouble* card. Who knew?"

"Don't gloat, Jackson," Josie said, frowning at him. "It's not becoming."

"Too late," he said.

Chapter 33

"You're joking, right?" I said, staring at the short skirt and heels Josie was wearing along with a white silk blouse that had a deep V cut from the shoulders. The outfit was stunning on her, but very much out of character. To use a musical analogy, her style of dress usually reminded me of a stylish jazz club. Smooth and cool, yet understated. Tonight's choice was like the brass fanfare surrounding the opening of a new Broadway musical.

"How is the poor guy supposed to focus on work tonight? Are you trying to seduce him or just torture him?"

"Definitely the latter," she said. "This is what Jackson gets for conning a date out of me the way he did."

"Well, you have to give him points for creativity and tenacity," I said, continuing to marvel at the way she looked.

"Yeah, maybe a couple," she said, draping a flowered scarf over her shoulders. "You look great."

"Thanks," I said, glancing in the mirror. My outfit was an upgrade over my tee shirt and sweats, although not nearly as comfortable.

I heard the knock on the door and went into the kitchen to greet Sammy. He'd agreed to watch Chloe even though she was well past the stage where she needed adult supervision. But I just hated leaving her alone.

"Hey, Suzy," Sammy said, leaning down to pet Chloe. "You look great. You got a hot date?"

"I seriously doubt it," I said, heading back into the living room.

Sammy followed me and stopped dead in his tracks when he got a look at Josie. I watched him do his best not to stare at her and then started laughing.

"Are you going to be okay, Sammy?" I said.

"Wh-what?" he said, glancing at me. "Yeah, I'm fine." Then his eyes locked back on Josie. "Geez, Doc. You look amazing."

"Thanks, Sammy," she said, casually accepting the compliment.

I knew it wasn't even close to being the last one she got tonight.

"I'm sorry for staring," he said. "It's just that I get so used to seeing you in those baggy scrubs all day I tend to forget what an incredibly tight package you come wrapped in."

Josie stared at him, looked at me with a bewildered expression, and then back at him with a hard glare.

"What did you say?" Josie whispered.

"Uh, sorry, Doc," he stammered. "That came out wrong. It was supposed to be a compliment."

"Maybe for a stripper on a pole," she said. "The tight package I come wrapped in? You know better than that, Sammy."

He stared down at the floor, his lighthearted mood shattered.

"You know, Sammy," Josie said, softening her tone a bit. "I've been wondering why such a good looking kid like you never seems to go out on any dates. I think I just figured it out. Keep going around talking about women like they're a piece of meat, and I swear I will make it my personal mission to make sure you die a lonely man."

"I'm sorry, Doc," he said. "It won't happen again."

"You're better than that, Sammy," Josie said, adjusting her scarf. "Let me clue you in on a little secret. The way to get a woman's attention, especially women like Suzy and me, is to focus on the things that make us interesting as human beings. And while we fully expect you to notice and appreciate the way we look, keep your comments about our *package* to yourself, no matter how incredibly tight it is. Am I making myself clear?"

"I got it, Josie. I'm so sorry."

221

"Okay. Enjoy your evening," she said, heading for the door.

"She's really mad at me, isn't she?" Sammy asked me when Josie was out of earshot.

"A little," I said. "But it's more disappointment than anything else."

"That's even worse," he said, sitting down on the couch.

"Yup," I said, grabbing my purse. "And that's another lesson worth learning early on."

I reached down to rub Chloe's head and waved goodbye to the forlorn young man staring off into space.

I walked outside and met Josie who was standing outside the SUV waiting for me to unlock it.

"Do you think I was too hard on him?" she said.

"No, he deserved it," I said. "And I doubt he'll be doing it again, so you probably did him a favor. Not to mention all the other women of Clay Bay."

"He's a good kid," she said. "But that comment ticked me off."

"I could tell," I said, unlocking the SUV. "Now are you going to be able to climb into your seat in that outfit, or do you need some help getting your incredibly tight package into the car?"

"Suzy?"

"Yes," I said, chuckling.

"Shut up."

We made the short drive to Tondeuse in under ten minutes and discovered Jackson already there and leaning against the side of his car in the parking lot.

"Hi, guys," he said, giving both of us the once over. "You look terrific."

I don't know if his intuition was working overtime tonight, but I knew he scored a point for not making any specific reference to Josie's outfit. I waited a few minutes until they had gone inside and got settled in at the bar, then walked inside and was greeted by the hostess. She escorted me to my table and Jerry the Lawyer stood as I approached.

He thought about going in for a hug, but stopped himself and settled for a handshake. His loss, I probably would have been okay with it.

"I was surprised to hear from you," he said. "You know, what with everything that's been going on with Rosaline."

"How is she doing?" I said, draping the napkin across my lap.

"Not good," he said. "This is the worst one yet."

I sensed him kicking himself under the table for the comment.

"There's been more than one?" I said, trying to sound casual.

He paused, then nodded and continued. "Yeah, there have."

"Since you've been dating?"

"Dating? That's not the word I'd use to describe it."

"What would you call it?"

"Providing protective services is probably the best term to use," he said, shrugging.

"You lost me, Jerry," I said, glancing around the room. At a nearby table, I recognized the state policeman who had been working on the murder case with Jackson. He was sitting with three other people I assumed were also cops.

"It's a long story," Jerry said.

"All the good ones are," I said, glancing up at the waitress who arrived with a glass of wine for me and a refill of Jerry's cocktail. "We're going to need a few minutes."

The waitress smiled and walked away. I looked at Jerry and waited.

"I don't know what to do, Suzy," he whispered.

Gone was the cocky, self-important lawyer I'd met on our first date. I looked across the table and saw a sad and lost little boy.

"All I wanted to do was to buy a boat and live on the beach," he said, swirling the ice cubes in his drink.

"It's not too late," I said.

"Oh, it's way too late," he said. "I'm probably on my way to jail for a very long time."

I felt my stomach jump, and I snuck a quick glance at the four cops sitting nearby just to make sure they were still there.

"Don't worry, Suzy," he said, forcing a laugh. "You're completely safe. I would never hurt you. In fact, I'd never hurt anybody. And Jackson and Josie in the bar and the four cops sitting at the table over there can all relax."

He took a sip from his drink and then took a deep breath.

"You know, I was about to turn myself in when you called. I agreed to come to dinner because it might be the last chance I get to talk to you and try to explain what's been going on. Since you were the only one able to do something about Rosaline, I figured it was the least I could do. I certainly wasn't able to do anything with her."

Stunned by his revelation and understanding of the situation he was in, I shifted in my seat, placed my elbows on the table and leaned closer.

"Rosaline killed Mr. and Mrs. Crawford, didn't she?" I whispered.

"Yes, she certainly did. And she tried her best to do the same to Roxanne. How's she doing anyway?"

"They think she's going to make it." I picked up my wine glass and then set it right back down because my hand was trembling.

"Good. I'm glad to hear that," Jerry said, draining half his drink.

"But you and Rosaline had an airtight alibi for all three. You were at the motel having... well, you know. Everyone heard the racket you two were making."

Jerry laughed.

"Yeah, it was loud. When Rosaline mentioned it, I thought she was crazy for thinking it would work. Well, she *is* crazy. But I thought the idea was just goofy. Boy, was I wrong. It worked like a charm. I should have known it would. All of Rosaline's schemes work. At least they did until now."

"I don't understand," I said, my hand finally settled enough for me to take a small sip of wine.

"It was a recording we made in New York a couple of months ago. We were sitting around her apartment when she brought it up. I should have put a stop to it right there. But I wasn't strong enough," he said, shrugging. "She put it on a loop that just kept repeating until we got back to the motel and turned it off."

"What?"

"Yeah, it's us on the tape faking it. We made sure that the manager had seen her enough times hanging around the motel. And we always made a point of being affectionate with each other when other people were around. She'd call when she was about to need an alibi, and I'd turn the tape on and start building the cover story."

"It sounds like a lot of trouble to go to," I said.

"Working for Crawford all those years taught Rosaline about the importance of details and having the ability to deflect attention away from her when it was necessary. If it came down to our word against the cops, who knows how well that would have help up. But as soon as the motel manager confirmed our alibi with specific details we were covered."

"You're saying you and Rosaline weren't dating?"

"No, we most certainly were not dating," he said, apparently finding the idea abhorrent.

"Why on earth not?"

225

"I suppose I could try and say something clever like I don't date crazy women or something like that. But let's stick with the truth."

"Which is?" I said, feeling like I was about to burst from anticipation.

"Rosaline is my sister."

I sat back in my chair and stared across the table at him in stunned silence.

"Didn't see that one coming, huh?" he said, finishing the rest of his drink.

"But how is that possible? I read every article about what happened with your family, and there was no reference to a son. Or brother."

"That's because I was given up for adoption at birth," he said, his eyes welling up with tears.

"Why on earth would your parents do something crazy like that?" I said, truly bewildered by the direction the conversation had turned.

"Well, for one, as I've discovered, crazy runs in my family. But the primary reason was that I wasn't my father's son."

I sat back in my chair as I processed the news.

"Your mother had an affair and your supposed father forced her to give you up?" I whispered.

"Yeah," he said, exhaling loudly. "It turns out he wasn't the forgiving type. And I'm sure that's where Rosaline gets it."

"I'm stunned," I said. I had tried for insightful but had to settle for stating the obvious.

"Oh, it gets better," he said, toying with his napkin. "Guess who my real father is?"

I sat quietly thinking about the question. Then the lightbulb went off.

"Bob Crawford?"

"The one and only."

"He met your mother when he was trying to buy your father's maple syrup company."

"You're good," Jerry said.

"And when he found out, he freaked out?"

"According to Rosaline, yes."

"But after all that, why on earth did he agree to sell his company to Crawford?"

"He didn't. But with all the lawyers hovering and my mom threatening to leave him for Crawford if he didn't agree to the sale, he eventually caved."

"This is unbelievable," I said, shaking my head.

"And then one night he finally lost it and... well, you know the rest of the story."

"But how did you reenter the picture?"

"Rosaline tracked me down about four years ago."

I sat in stunned silence again trying to process what I'd just learned.

"I guess that wouldn't have been too hard," I said. "All Rosaline needed to do was track down the family that adopted you."

"That's what she thought," Jerry said, sliding his menu to the other side of the table. "But what Rosaline didn't know was that my adoptive family gave me up when I was three."

"What?"

"Yeah, apparently they had a change of heart at some point. It turns out I was an overactive child with a fondness for fire. They couldn't deal with me. So I began a thirteen-year odyssey through the Canadian and U.S. foster systems."

I felt my bottom lip begin to quiver.

"How many different families were there?"

"Eight," he said. "Six in Canada and two more here in the States. When I turned sixteen, I got my driver's license and just took off on my own. I had no idea where I would end up, but I knew it had to be better than where I was."

"So where did you go?"

He took a sip of his fresh cocktail.

"I'd saved enough money to buy a new identity, added a couple of years to my age, and joined the military. The tests they gave me showed that I had an aptitude for finance, and when I got out I went straight to college and got my degree in three years. Three years after that, I got my law degree. And now... well, here I am. Jerry the Lawyer."

"You didn't know you were Crawford's son did you?"

"Not a clue. Not until Rosaline managed to track me down."

"How did she find you?" I said, hanging on every word.

"The usual stuff. Contacts with the various foster homes. Private investigators. And once they made the connection with the name change, it was pretty simple from there."

"So the whole thing about you helping Mrs. Crawford out with her finances was an elaborate setup?" I said.

"Yeah, that was just one more piece of Rosaline's long-term plan," he said, trailing his finger down his water glass that was beading with icy drops of water.

I watched and waited out the silence.

"But don't get me wrong," he said as a thought entered his head. "I'm really good at what I do, so it wasn't that much of a con job on Mrs. Crawford. And you don't have anything to worry about. I did a really good job with your mom's stuff."

I nodded and snuck a glance at the table full of cops sitting nearby. They were paying close attention while trying not to be obvious about it, and

228

I wondered if some form of listening device had been hidden somewhere on or under our table. I started tapping my spoon on the table and saw one of the cops touch her ear. Normally I would have been pleased with that successful piece of detective work, but I took no pleasure from it. All I felt was an overwhelming sadness for the lost man sitting across from me.

"So Rosaline had a long-term plan to, what, infiltrate Crawford and his company by getting hired and working her way up?"

"Yeah," Jerry said. "She thought once I was identified as Crawford's son, as the sole heir, I'd have a good shot at inheriting all of it."

"It might have worked," I said.

"Yeah, I think it would have. Of course, Rosaline expected me to pick her to run the whole thing. Rosaline's focus is unbelievable, and once she sets a goal, if you know what's good for you, all you can do is get out of her way."

"And then you signed up to help her?"

"No," he said, shaking his head. "After she told me what her plan was, I played along to see if I could stop her."

"From killing Crawford?"

"At first that was the goal. Then she started worrying about Mrs. Crawford coming back into the picture. When that happened, both of the Crawford's had to go."

"Revenge, right?"

"Of course. She blamed Crawford for the destruction of our family. What there was of it," he said, forcing a small laugh. "Along the way it got tempered with greed and ego, but it was a revenge play from the start."

"I'm confused about the timing. Why was it so important to do it now?"

"That was me," he said, swirling his ice cubes then taking another sip. He looked at his glass. "I wonder how long it's going to be before I get to

229

have another one of these." Then he brightened and gave me a strange smile that made me nervous. "Maybe I'll get put in a minimum security prison that has a Happy Hour." Then he cackled and downed the rest of his drink.

Hmmm. Maybe it did run in the family.

"What did you do?" I said, desperate to get back on topic before he decided that maybe he'd said enough.

"I thought it was an elegant plan," he said, laughing softly. "Boy, was I wrong."

I was on the edge of my seat and at one point had to catch myself from falling forward off my chair. But I bit my tongue and continued to wait out the long silences.

"I sent Crawford a key in the mail along with an anonymous note that said he and I needed to meet. I put just enough cryptic information in the note to let him know that I had some very incriminating evidence about his past."

"He didn't know that you were his son, did he?"

"No, absolutely not. But I was going to tell Crawford when we met," he said. "I needed to see his reaction."

"Did you ever get the chance to meet with him?"

"No, before I could get a meeting set up the dummy blew a gasket and told Rosaline, his ex-wife, and Roxanne about the key and the note."

"Why would he do that?" I noticed the waitress approaching our table and motioned for another round of drinks.

"Like I said, my note rattled his cage. Maybe he thought it was about the Sugarland sale and everything that went along with that. My guess is that he told Rosaline because he was concerned the information might have something to do with the company. He probably told Mrs. Crawford because he thought she might be behind the whole thing. And given Roxanne's history, he could have been worried about some skeletons in her closet that would embarrass him and make the shareholders nervous." He looked at me and shrugged. "Who knows? All of them certainly had reasons to be nervous and the uncertainty of what it was drove them all nuts. Especially Rosaline."

"You didn't tell her it was you, right?"

"Suzy, if I had, I'd be a dead man."

I swallowed hard.

"But why did you do it?"

"She's my sister. I hoped I could save Rosaline from herself. Over the past year, she's turned really erratic and extremely dangerous," he whispered. "Crazy plan, huh?"

"Yeah, pretty much," I said, nodding.

He managed a small laugh.

"Like I said, it runs in the family."

"Have you been diagnosed with anything?"

"Oh, I have a few minor issues that I need to keep an eye on, but mine lean toward wounds of a self-inflicted nature."

"Why are you telling me all of this?"

"Because it's time," he said. "And you're the only one I feel comfortable telling."

"I don't think I can help you, Jerry."

"I'm not looking for help," he said, his eyes flaring briefly. "I'm telling you because you're the only one who will listen." He leaned forward and gave me a hard stare.

"Relax, Jerry," I whispered. "I'm listening."

"Sorry," he said. "This is all just too much stress and guilt to deal with."

"I understand. At least I'm trying."

231

"Anyway, after Crawford spilled the beans about the key and the note, Rosaline came up with the idea for Crawford to take a break and spend some time on the island."

"And you figured out a way to tag along?"

"Yeah, I figured she'd get into all sorts of trouble if I weren't around. Obviously, it didn't make a bit of difference whether I was here or not."

"Apart from giving her an airtight alibi," I blurted.

"Yeah, I did do that, didn't I?" he said, thinking about it, then shrugging it off.

"Please tell me you weren't involved in the murders."

"Not directly. It was always after the fact."

"And the maple syrup was... what? Some weird tribute to the memory of her father?"

"It was something like that. Rosaline said she poured a gallon of it down Crawford's throat before she threw him overboard."

"How the heck did she manage to do that?"

"She slipped him a couple of her own pills. Rosaline is on some pretty serious medications to help control her mood swings. Crawford nodded off during their boat ride. She pulled the maple syrup trick, tossed him overboard, and then went looking for the dog. But the dog must have figured it out and jumped in the water before she could get her hands on it."

An intense loathing for the woman flooded through me.

"When Rosaline flips her crazy switch on, there's no way of telling what she might do," Jerry said.

I flashed back to the damage she'd inflicted on her car when she'd discovered the four flat tires and nodded in silent agreement.

"And Mrs. Crawford?" I said.

"You mean, why kill her now?"

"Yeah."

232

"Well, as I'm sure you noticed at dinner that night, they hated each other. And once the rumor of a possible Crawford reconciliation started swirling around, Rosaline was scared to death that Mrs. Crawford would figure out a way to get her out of the company. When the opportunity presented itself, she just went for it."

"And she figured out a way to set Chef Claire up for the murder," I said.

"Rosaline called taking Mrs. Crawford out and getting Chef Claire blamed for it a two for one," he said, shaking his head. "She found out that Chef Claire had been seeing Carl and was enraged by the thought of it."

"Really? I wouldn't have thought that Carl was anything more than a temporary plaything for Rosaline."

"He wasn't. But Rosaline isn't very good at sharing her toys," Jerry said.

"But she knew that Roxanne had also been sleeping with Carl, right?"

"Yes," he said, smiling. "But Roxanne's infidelity was something Rosaline thought she might be able to use to her advantage at some point in the future. So she encouraged Roxanne to go for it."

"But then she changed her mind and tried to kill her?" I said, shaking my head. "It doesn't make any sense."

"Suzy, you need to remember that we are talking about a sick and very dangerous individual here. I haven't talked with Rosaline since she attacked Roxanne, but my guess is that Rosaline went to that house with the intention of killing Carl, not Roxanne. She was just unlucky enough to be there when Rosaline showed up."

"And Rosaline had already flipped on her crazy switch," I said.

"Yes, I'm sure she had."

"Josie and I almost got run over by another boat the night we had dinner at the island. That was Rosaline, wasn't it?"

233

"No," Jerry said, shaking his head. "That was Roxanne. After you had left, she and Mrs. Crawford got into a screaming match, and Roxanne took off in one of the boats just to get away for a while. She didn't even know how to turn the lights on, let alone drive it. She was lucky she made it back alive. I guess you guys were pretty lucky, too."

Exhausted, I sat back in my chair.

"The key is for a safe deposit box, isn't it?"

Jerry nodded.

"Do you mind telling me what's in it?" I said.

"I thought if I put together enough information from different sources I could convince Crawford that everyone had a lot to lose if it all came out. And I was going to try to have the same conversation with Rosaline. And Mrs. Crawford if it came to that. It was a crazy idea, but I figured that if nobody could come out a winner, then maybe the whole thing could be put to rest and everyone could just move on. And with the right help, maybe Rosaline could get better."

"Boy, were you wrong," I deadpanned.

Jerry laughed long and hard.

"Yeah, I definitely whiffed on that one, didn't I?" he said, rubbing his forehead.

"So what's in the safe deposit box?"

"There's a copy of Rosaline's complete psychiatric history I was able to get my hands on. Don't ask me how. I can't divulge where I got it because it would create enormous problems for the person who gave it to me."

I nodded and waited.

"And there are a lot of Mr. and Mrs. Crawford's financial transactions. Many of them tawdry. Some of them highly illegal."

"And nothing they'd want to read about in the newspaper."

234

"Correct. The other item in the box is my mom's diary," he said, staring off into the distance. "She kept a very detailed journal about her life that includes the history of her affair with Crawford, her thoughts about being a mother, and a host of other things that aren't flattering to anyone. I was devastated when I read it."

"Where on earth did you get your hands on that?"

"The private investigator who eventually tracked me down found it in an evidence box at the police station in Smithville. They were the ones who investigated the murder-suicide, and it was an open and shut case and such a horrific story for a small town like that to deal with, they just took a bunch of stuff from the house, stuffed it into some boxes, and tried to forget all about it. The PI took the diary without anyone noticing and gave it to me when we met. She thought I should have it. I guess she took pity on me. Either that or she knew that Rosaline would go completely off the tracks if she ever saw it."

"So Rosaline doesn't know about the diary?"

"No," he said, leaning forward to grasp my hands. This time, I squeezed back. "And whatever happens, you have to promise me that she never will."

"Okay," I said, my voice cracking. "I'll do my best."

"But I guess I don't have to worry about that," he said, letting go of my hands and sitting back in his chair. "The key's disappeared. I guess it's probably somewhere at the bottom of the River."

"Uh, actually," I said, coughing nervously. "I have it."

"What?"

"I mean I did have it. I turned it over to the cops."

"Where on earth did you find it?"

"It was sewn into Chloe's collar," I said.

"Serves me right for not being a dog lover," he said, shaking his head. "Wow. That changes things."

"So where's this safe deposit box?"

"You were just there," he said.

"Smithville?"

"Yup. Smithville First National. I thought that hiding it there provided perfect symmetry."

I reached down and entered KMN and sent the text to Josie. Moments later she and Jackson strolled out of the bar and headed our way.

"Well, I'll be," Jackson said, trying to feign surprise and failing miserably. "Look who's here."

"Don't worry about the charade, Jackson. Just have a seat," I said.

"Hi, Chief," Jerry said, gesturing to the empty chair next to him. "Hello, Josie. I'd tell you how beautiful you look tonight, but by now you're probably tired of hearing that."

"See?" Josie said, smiling at Jackson. "That's how it's done."

Jackson flushed with embarrassment.

"Let's have a drink," Jerry said.

"Are you okay?" Jackson said me.

"Yeah," I said. "Actually, I'm feeling pretty good."

Jerry and I smiled at each other. It was an odd moment, and I was convinced the evening couldn't get any stranger.

Then Jerry turned to the table of four cops sitting nearby and pointed at our table.

"Would you folks care to join us for a cocktail?" he said, sliding his chair toward Jackson.

The four cops looked at each other, then shrugged and pulled their chairs up to our table. And for the next two hours, five cops, a man about to be charged with accessory to murder, and the bewildered owners of the

236

Thousand Islands Doggy Inn, drank, occasionally laughed, and wondered aloud what the future might hold.

And about my earlier comment regarding how the evening couldn't get any stranger?

Boy, was I wrong.

Epilogue

Things settled down around town after that and Josie and I got a chance to focus on our dogs instead of murder. As much as I love a good mystery, it was a welcome change. And Chloe continues to grow like a weed and is pretty much the center of my social life. But I'm keeping my fingers crossed on that front.

Rosaline's trial was quick but eventful. During sentencing, as Josie likes to say, she completely lost the plot and tried to climb the judge's bench and beat him with his gavel. Rosaline was subdued, sedated, and then sentenced in absentia to spend the rest of her life in a very secure facility for the criminally insane.

But her mother's diary never surfaced at her trial. I owe Jackson big time for that one.

Jerry the Lawyer pled guilty to accessory to the two murders, but due to his life story and some other mitigating factors, he only received a ten-year sentence with the possibility of parole after five. Maybe he will get the chance to open his charter fishing business after all.

Roxanne, while still hobbled, is going to make a full recovery. Every time she sees us, she makes it a point to apologize for almost killing us that night on the River. We've forgiven her, but she still hasn't been able to forgive herself. She and Carl are joined at the hip and planning to open an exotic flower business in town. I'm still waiting to see if it's possible for orchids to bloom in the Thousand Islands in February, but I'm keeping my fingers crossed for them. Josie gives it a year; the flower business, not their relationship. She gives that six months.

238

Sammy decided that he'd like to pursue a career working with animals and has joined our staff on a full-time basis. Josie has a feeling he might not have the intellectual chops to get into vet school, but she does concede that since he has stopped making frat jokes and crude observations about women, at least in our presence, he has demonstrated a willingness and ability to learn.

As I predicted, my mother's relationship with the veterinarian flamed out. She was already starting to get bored with him and his *incessant prattling* about various animal surgeries he'd performed over the years. But the last flicker of light burned out one evening when she'd gone in for a romantic hug a little too quickly, and his overprotective Rottweiler had nipped her hand. So it was back into the dating pool for Mom. Now she's active on seven different online dating sites and driving a new Porsche. But she's only dating on this side of the border. She still hasn't quite worked up enough nerve to go back to Canada.

Jackson and Freddie, our medical examiner extraordinaire, continue their energetic, yet fruitless, pursuit of Josie who continues to deflect their affections with a gentle smile. As they both should have figured out by now, if either one of them had a shot with her, she would have let them know by now. But it is a lot of fun watching them fall over themselves trying and if it makes them happy, knock yourself out, guys.

Chef Claire was released and set free of all charges. Since she was unsure about what she wanted to do next, we invited her to stay with us at the house until she figured it out. Given her cooking skills, she can take all the time she wants.

But at the moment, I'm hoping she hurries up. She promised to make breakfast before the three of us head out on the River to enjoy a beautiful fall day. The leaves are turning and the weather, while cooling down, is perfect for a boat ride and maybe a little fishing if the mood strikes. While waiting, I

239

packed a picnic basket, and Chloe kept a close eye on me to make sure I didn't forget her apple slices.

Josie entered the kitchen, picked Chloe up for a good morning hug, something that was getting harder to do on a daily basis, then set her down and poured herself a cup of coffee.

"It's a beautiful day to be out on the River," she said.

I nodded as I stared out the window at the dark blue water accented by the red and yellow foliage.

"Life is good," Josie said, taking a sip of coffee. "But your coffee still needs a lot of work."

I punched her gently on the arm and noticed Chef Claire coming down the stairs.

"Good morning," I said. "Nice to see you."

"I know, I know," she said, laughing. "I'm late getting breakfast started."

"There's no hurry," I said, feeling my stomach rumble.

"Speak for yourself," Josie said.

I glanced out through the window when I heard the UPS truck pull into the driveway.

"Are we expecting a package?" I said.

"I don't think so," Josie said.

The driver climbed the stairs, and I greeted him at the door and signed for the box. I set it down on the table and checked the address. It was mailed from Smithville.

"I wonder what it is," I said, tearing open the box.

Inside the carefully wrapped package were a solitary glass bottle and a handwritten note. I turned the bottle around and laughed when I saw the label.

240

"Well, would you look at that? A bottle of the famous Sugarland Farms syrup," I said, opening the note. It read as follows:

Dear ladies,

I was in my downstairs cellar the other day making room for my new batch of preserves when I found this bottle tucked away in a corner. It's never been opened, and I don't think maple syrup that's been properly stored ever goes bad, but I'll leave that decision up to you. At a minimum, I thought you might like the bottle as a reminder.

I've been following the Crawford events closely and reprinting some of the stories in the Gazette given the Smithville connection. I'm glad that it's been resolved and that you're both safe and sound.

And if you ever make your way back to our little town, please make sure you drop by and say hello. Wishing you the best.

Liz Johnson

"What a sweet thing to do. She's such a nice woman," Josie said, examining the bottle. "What do you think?"

"About eating it? I'm not sure. It has to be thirty years old," I said, glancing at Chef Claire.

"I think it might be okay," Chef Claire said. "And we'll know as soon as we open it if it isn't."

"I'm willing to give it a shot," I said. "After all, it's the least we can do since we've heard so much about how good it is."

"I suppose I could whip up a batch of French toast," Chef Claire said.

"The kind where you toss the blueberries into the batter?" I said.

"That's the one," Chef Claire said.

"With bacon wrapped sausage?" I said, glancing at Josie.

"Sure, why not?" Chef Claire said, laughing.

241

"What do you say, Josie?" I said, sitting down at the table.

Josie sat down, nodded her head vigorously, and rolled up her sleeves.

"I could eat."

Here's an excerpt from the next installment in B.R. Snow's *Thousand Islands Doggy Inn Mystery* series:

The Case of the
Brokenhearted Bulldog

Chapter 1

I stretched out on one of the lounge chairs surrounding the massive swimming pool. Being late September, the pool was empty, and I knew that after this annual end of summer soiree ended, the pool would be covered and the lounge chairs stored away until May. Or if winter behaved like the last person at a party who refused to take the hint and leave, the chairs might not make another appearance until June.

Chloe, my gorgeous Australian Shepherd Josie and I had rescued from the River a few months ago, took my prone position as an invitation to climb up on my full stomach and stretch out. I groaned from her weight, but couldn't say no to her. I pulled myself into more or less an upright position and Chloe took the hint, moved down, and repositioned herself until she was draped over my legs. She propped her head on top of her crossed front paws and surveyed the scene.

A couple of hundred people filled the lawn of the Clay Bay Yacht Club. It was an interesting mix of locals, summer residents, and boat owners and their crew about to depart for warmer climates. Dozens of dogs mingled through the crowd on the prowl for food and friendship. I surveyed the scene and reviewed my notes for the speech I had to make later. I hated public speaking more than just about anything, but since John Gordon, owner of Gordon Yachts and president of the Clay Bay Yacht Club, always included a fundraising component for the Thousand Islands Doggy Inn rescue program as part of his annual end of summer party, it was the least I could do.

This year, John had donated a brand new fishing boat that retailed north of a hundred thousand dollars. And all summer people had been buying five dollar raffle tickets for a chance at winning it. As of this morning, the total number of tickets sold hit the thirty thousand mark. A hundred and fifty thousand dollars would shelter and feed a lot of dogs, and we owed John big time. A three-minute speech to thank him for all his support barely scratched the surface.

But that didn't make the thought of speaking in public any more appealing. Or less frightening. I shuffled my note cards, put them back in my pocket, and stroked Chloe's head. She closed her eyes, and I was about to do the same when Josie, my best friend and business partner, wandered in my direction.

As always, every pair of eyes she walked past followed her movements. A man I didn't recognize continued to stare at Josie as he walked with his wife along the edge of the pool and almost fell in. His wife grabbed his sleeve at the last minute, and he successfully windmilled his arms until he caught his balance. She seemed to regret saving him from the cold water because she scowled and left her embarrassed husband standing by himself.

I stifled my laughter, but Josie hadn't seen any of it. Her focus was on the heaping plate of food she was carrying. She plopped down on the lounge chair next to mine and settled in. Chloe shifted positions and stared intensely at Josie's plate.

"Sorry, Chloe," Josie said, reaching over to stroke her head. "This is people food."

Chloe barked once. She knew exactly what Josie was saying, but she didn't like what she was hearing.

Josie and I laughed. Chloe kept staring at the plate, but Josie was resolute. Chloe woofed one more time, but her heart wasn't in it. She was beaten, and she knew it.

"Chef Claire outdid herself," Josie said. "These barbecue shrimp are amazing. Did you try them?" She devoured another one, then caught the expression on my face. "Dumb question. Forget I even asked."

Josie momentarily forgot my deep and unabiding commitment to avoid eating anything that comes from the water; either salt or fresh. But since she's in the process of working her way into an appetizer-induced coma, I'll forgive her temporary loss of memory.

"I know you must have gone to town on the cheesesteak sliders," she said, grabbing a deep-fried stuffed mushroom from her plate.

"Yes," I said, rubbing my stomach. "And the mushrooms, the Italian sausage and peppers, and the chicken-corn fritters."

"Did you try the bacon-wrapped figs stuffed with blue cheese?"

"Yeah," I said, holding my stomach. "I had a couple."

Josie raised an eyebrow at me as she chewed.

"Define a couple," she said.

"Eight. Maybe ten."

"Lightweight," she said, selecting another shrimp from her plate.

She held the plate out toward me. I shook my head and continued to rub my stomach.

"Okay," Josie said. "More for me."

Her ability to consume prodigious amounts of food without gaining a pound continued to baffle me. I'd made a solid effort today to keep up with her, but who was I kidding? If she hadn't decided to become a veterinarian, she would have had a bright future as a competitive eater.

"It's a nice turnout," Josie said. "John's gone above and beyond what anybody could expect."

"He certainly has," I said. "Have you seen him yet?"

"Only briefly," she said. "He seemed a bit distracted, but he's probably just trying to get everything wrapped up for the season."

"Yeah, I'm sure he is," I said, glancing down at Chloe who was focused on something on the other side of the lawn.

"But he did say he had a surprise for later on," Josie said, setting her empty plate on a nearby table.

"There's more?" I said.

"Apparently," she said, then stopped.

I heard her trying to swallow a gasp and followed her eyes to the other side of the lawn.

I recognized the man strolling our way along with a massive dog. They were both drawing a lot of attention and their progress toward us was slow.

"Who on earth is that?" Josie said, staring intensely at the man.

"That is the famous Summerman Lawless," I said, climbing out of the lounge chair. "And the dog is Murray."

"He's magnificent," Josie said.

"Are you referring to him or the dog?"

"What dog?" Josie asked.

I stared at her. It didn't happen very often. In fact, I'd only see it three times before. But there was no mistaking what I was witnessing. Josie's motor was running full throttle.

"You said he's famous?" she said, unable to take her eyes off the man who continued to make his way across the lawn.

"He's a musician originally from the area. Do you remember the band Life's Eclectic Nightmare?"

"LEN? Sure, I remember them. Aren't they the ones who died in a boating accident?"

"Everyone in the band except for one member. That's him," I said, waving to him.

"What's he doing here?" Josie said, clambering out of her lounge chair to stand next to me.

"He's got an island a couple of miles downriver. He tries to get to the River each summer, but I haven't seen him around this year."

"You know this man?" Josie asked, staring at me.

"Sure, I've known him for years," I said, shrugging. "He was ahead of me at school, but he's pretty tight with my mom. I had such a crush on him when I was younger."

"I'd be shocked if you hadn't," Josie said.

Murray spotted me and made a beeline for us. Chloe, completely unsure about what to do about the massive beast, barked, and then sat down near my feet and cocked her head. Murray stood on his back legs and gently placed his front paws on my shoulders.

"Hello, Murray," I said, vigorously rubbing his massive head.

Murray glanced down and spotted Chloe. They spent the next few minutes checking each other out, decided they liked each other and began playing and rolling in the grass.

"What a great dog," Josie said, apparently noticing the gigantic beast for the first time.

"Hi, Suzy. So good to see you."

"Hi, Summerman," I said, giving him a hug. "Where have you been all summer?"

"It's a long story," he said.

"All the good ones are," I said.

"Yeah, you're right. I spent most of the summer bouncing back and forth between Vegas and China."

"Well, I'm glad you made it here today," I said.

"John's making me sing for my supper," he said, laughing. "But for you and your rescue program, I'm happy to do it."

"You're going to play?" I said. "That's great."

I felt a small kick on my ankle and heard Josie's soft cough.

"Summerman, I'd like you to meet my best friend and business partner, Josie."

"Oh, yes. You're the vet I've heard so much about," he said, extending his hand. "It's nice to meet you."

"The pleasure is all mine," Josie said.

I glanced at the expression on her face and shook my head.

"Do I need to get the hose?" I whispered.

"I'm a huge fan," she said, ignoring me.

I grinned and glanced down at the lawn to hide it. Josie was gushing, and I made a mental note to remind her about it later. And the only thing that was huge around here at the moment, apart from Murray, was the lie she'd just told him. Josie spent about as much time listening to music as I did eating fish.

"Tell me about this magnificent animal," Josie said, kneeling to rub Murray's head. "A Newfie, Golden Retriever mix, right?"

"Very good. Most people don't get it on their first guess."

"Well, I'm a vet, so…"

"Interesting," Summerman said, studying Josie closely.

I'm sure he thought Josie was incredibly interesting, but he was playing it very cool. Josie was so used to deflecting the attentions of men she didn't find interesting, now that she was playing the role of pursuer and not getting the reaction she might have expected, she seemed unsure of herself. So for the moment Josie continued to focus on the dog.

When in doubt, play to your strengths.

"The woman who breeds them, calls them Goldenlands," Summerman said.

"I've never seen one," Josie said, putting Murray into a leg kicking trance as she scratched his stomach. "In fact, I've never even heard of the breed."

"Yeah, I'm not big on sharing them," he said, petting Chloe.

Josie, confused, stared at him. It was the first time any expression other than unbridled lust had crossed her face for several minutes.

"I own all of them," he continued.

"I don't understand," Josie said. "You own the entire breed?"

"The breeder is the only one I've found anywhere, so I pay her a lot of money to take care of all of them and keep them off the market. Except for the one that's currently under your spell," he said, laughing. "Consider yourself lucky, Murray. I'd need to have four legs to get one of those."

"Don't bet on it," I whispered, then flinched from the quick punch to my knee Josie delivered.

"Most rock stars collect things like houses and cars," he said. "I collect these guys. Weird, huh?"

"Maybe a little," I said. "But if you ever change your mind, I'll be more than happy to take a couple off your hands."

"I don't know if my breeder friend would appreciate that. She's pretty happy spending all day surrounded by unconditional love. But I'm sure I don't have to explain that to you guys."

"No," I said, nodding. "We get that one. Right, Josie?"

"Huh?" she said. "Oh, absolutely."

"Look, I need to run," Summerman said. "I need to do a quick sound check. But maybe I'll see you guys later."

"Absolutely," Josie said. "Maybe you could come over to the house for dinner sometime."

"I'd love too," he said. "But Murray and I are heading off tonight."

"Some people," I said, laughing. "The first day of fall arrives, and you're out of here like you got shot from a cannon."

"Well, Murray and I have a travel commitment we can't miss. Isn't that right, Murray?"

Murray woofed, and I swear he nodded his head.

"Okay," Summerman said. "I'll see you later. Suzy, great seeing you as always."

I moved in to accept his hug.

"Josie, it's been a pleasure meeting you," he said, extending his hand.

"Absolutely," she said, returning the handshake.

"You ready, Murray? Let's go see if we can find you a snack."

We returned his wave and watched them make their way back across the lawn. I snapped my fingers in front of Josie's face.

"Wow," she said, continuing to stare at them. "Is it my imagination or did I just make a complete fool of myself?"

"Absolutely," I said, laughing.

"Yeah, I was kind of repeating myself for a while there wasn't I?"

"Absolutely."

"Shut up," Josie said. Then she laughed and shook her head. "And to think I was beginning to wonder if my motor was still working."

"I'd say it's working fine," I said. "For a teenage girl anyway."

"Was I that bad?"

"Absolutely deplorable," I said, unable to stop laughing. "What do you have to say for yourself?"

"Woof."

Made in the USA
San Bernardino, CA
06 December 2016